D1470527

CARTEL PUBLICATIONS
PRESENTS
SILENCE
OF THE
NINE
III
T. STYLES
NATIONAL BESTSELLING AUTHOR OF RAUNCHY

ARE YOU ON OUR EMAIL LIST?

SIGN UP ON OUR WEBSITE

www.thecartelpublications.com

OR TEXT THE WORD:

CARTELBOOKS TO 22828

FOR PRIZES, CONTESTS, ETC.

Check out other titles by The Cartel Publications

Shyt List 1: Be Careful Who You Cross

Shyt List 2: Loose Cannon

Shyt List 3: And A Child Shall Leave Them

SHYT LIST 4: Children Of The Wronged

Shyt List 5: Smokin' Crazies The Finale'

Pitbulls in a Skirt 1

Pitbulls in a Skirt 2

Pitbulls In A Skirt 3: The Rise Of Lil C

Pitbulls In A Skirt 4: Killer Klan

Pitbulls In A Skirt 5: The Fall From Grace

Poison 1

Poison 2

Victoria's Secret

Hell Razor Honeys 1

Hell Razor honeys 2

Black and Ugly

Black and Ugly As Ever

Miss Wayne & The Queens of DC

A Hustler's Son

A Hustler's Son 2

The Face That Launched A Thousand Bullets

Year of the Crackmom

The Unusual Suspects

La Familia Divided

Raunchy

Raunchy 2: Mad's Love

Raunchy 3: Jayden's Passion

Mad Maxxx: Children of The Catacombs (Extra Raunchy)

Kali: Raunchy Relived: The Miller Family

Reversed

Quita's DayScare Center

Quita's DayScare Center 2

Dead Heads

Drunk & Hot Girls

Pretty Kings

Pretty Kings 2: Scarlett's Fever

 By T. STYLES

Pretty Kings 3: Denim's Blues

Pretty Kings 4: Race's Rage

Hersband Material

Upscale Kittens

Wake & Bake Boys

Young & Dumb

Young & Dumb: Vyce's Getback

Tranny 911

Tranny 911: Dixie's Rise

First Comes Love, Then Comes Murder

Luxury Tax

The Lying King

Crazy Kind of Love

Silence of The Nine

Silence of The Nine II: Let There Be Blood

Silence of The Nine III

Prison Throne

Goon

Hoetic Justice

And They Call Me God

The Ungrateful Bastards

Lipstick Dom

A School of Dolls

Skeezers

Skeezers 2

You Kissed Me Now I Own You

Nefarious

Redbone 3: The Rise Of The Fold

The Fold

Clown Niggas

The One You Shouldn't Trust

Cold As Ice

The Whore The Wind Blew My Way

She Brings The Worst Kind

The House That Crack Built

The House That Crack Built 2: Russo & Amina

The House That Crack Built 3: Reggie & Tamika

The End. How To Write A Bestselling Novel in 30 Days

WWW.THECARTELPUBLICATIONS.COM

SILENCE OF THE NINE 3:

BY

T. STYLES

PUBLISHER'S NOTE:
This book is a work of fiction. Names, characters, businesses,
Organizations, places, events and incidents are the product of the
Author's imagination or are used fictionally. Any resemblance of
Actual persons, living or dead, events, or locales are entirely coincidental.

Library of Congress Control Number: 2017964630

ISBN 10: 1945240903

ISBN 13: 978-1945240904

Cover Design: Davida Baldwin
www.oddballdsgn.com

www.thecartelpublications.com
First Edition
Printed in the United States of America

What's Up Fam,

I hope and pray each and every one of you reading this letter had a wonderful Christmas. Mine was full of love and happiness that the season should bring.

2018 is upon us and with the new year comes the 10 YEAR ANNIVERSAY of THE CARTEL PUBLICATIONS!! Yep, we entered into the literary scene in January 2008 and thanks to you extremely loyal readers, we are still here and stronger than ever! Get ready, because we turning the switch up on the game! We hope you continue to ride with us!

Now...Silence of The Nine 3! I don't even know where to begin. This one brings with it the elegance, grit, grossness and love that I have become accustomed to in reading this family saga. I couldn't put the book down until the last page and even then I wanted more! Cancel whatever plans you have made for today because you will be in for the night with this one!

With that being said, keeping in line with tradition, we want to give respect to a vet or trailblazer paving the way. In this novel, we would like to recognize:

Tiffany Haddish

Tiffany Sarac Haddish is an American comedian and actress. Although she has been in the game for years doing stand up and appearing on TV shows, she made her film breakthrough as Dina in the movie, "Girls Trip" where she stole the show. Tiffany has recently penned a novel, "The Last Black Unicorn" which is a hilarious and brutally honest insight on her life of love and loss. Make sure you check it out.

Aight, get to it. I'll catch you in the next book.

Be Easy!

Charisse "C. Wash" Washington

Vice President

The Cartel Publications

www.thecartelpublications.com

www.facebook.com/publishercwash

Instagram: publishercwash

www.twitter.com/cartelbooks

www.facebook.com/cartelpublications

Follow us on Instagram: Cartelpublications

#CartelPublications

#UrbanFiction

#PrayForCeCe

#TiffanyHaddish

CARTEL URBAN CINEMA'S WEB SERIES

BMORE CHICKS

@ Pink Crystal Inn

NOW AVAILABLE:

Via

YOUTUBE

And

DVD

(Season 2 Coming Spring 2018)

www.youtube.com/user/tstyles74

www.cartelurbancinema.com

www.thecartelpublications.com

#SilenceOfTheNine3

This is a family saga.

For your convenience the family tree can be found in the back of the novel.

"As men in rage strike those that wish them best..."

- **William Shakespeare** – *Othello*

PROLOGUE

Chained to thick wooden trellises used to upkeep the vineyard behind Aristocrat Hills, Nine begged for mercy from all who would listen. Completely naked, blood oozed from her beaten face, arms and thighs deepening the redness of the grapes surrounding her chocolate frame. Every so often lightning flashed across the sky brightening her beautiful but pummeled features; as thunder appeared to yell *fuck you* from above.

Through swollen eyes she could see that it was obvious that her perpetrators were not there to offer mercy, but to enact the brand of revenge they felt she deserved.

Taking a deep breath Nine looked above and said, "So this is really it for me."

"Shouldn't it be?" The perpetrator asked, pointing the barrel of a .45 at her as if it were a microphone. "Don't play the martyr, Nine. You have also killed many."

Her head hung low upon hearing the words. "This may be true. But it was always within the rules of the game. But this is different."

"Shut the fuck up!" The perpetrator grew louder. "Just shut up!"

Nine sighed deeply. "If this is it, let me say I'm sorry now for all the things I wanted to be for my sons but couldn't. And that if this be my final resting place then I will accept my fate because I am at home. But trust me, it may not be now or even this year, but you will soon receive yours." She glared.

As she looked outward, the pain of the betrayal she felt in her heart thickened by those whose blood coursed through her veins and whose hearts she thought she owned, she took a deep breath.

Realizing her fate, and with a resilience only Nine Prophet could muster she said, "If you're going to do it let's get it over with. I will beg no more."

CHAPTER ONE

NINE PROPHET

MANY MONTHS EARLIER

"For thou hast more of the wild-goose in one of thy wits than, I am sure, I have in my whole five."

- William Shakespeare

Draped in a long red dress that hugged her curvaceous but pregnant physique, Nine sat at the head of a long cherry wood table in the dining room at Aristocrat Hills. Bossed to perfection.

Her short black silky hair was teased just right causing her curls to open in tiny circles. Empty bottles of Francesca Merlot sat alongside crystal and gold goblets and the magnificent shine from the chandeliers above provided the room with a soft glow.

At the end of the day they looked like movie stars.

The Prophet name meant paper and this incestuous clan had much of it. And yet every dollar, every shiny cent, was handled by Nine.

"The world doesn't like us," Nine said massaging her large belly after feeling her and Leaf's child moving inside her womb. Her enormous diamond wedding ring as bright as a white halogen bulb. "And that is okay because their hate makes us stronger." She paused. "Just like that bitch Anna attempted to extort money by telling the world how we breed ended in vain, so will our enemies fall if we continue to stand together."

She stood up and moved around the table like a beautiful slithering snake. Surrounding it was her aunt and uncles, Lisa, Porter, Wagner and Jeremy who were Kerrick's illegitimate children who entered her life almost two years ago. Bridget, Kerrick's secret concubine who gave birth to them, was also present. On the other side of the table were her cousins Samantha, Noel and Bethany.

Everyone may have acted fake for the evening in their expensive black designer outfits as requested by Nine but many of the original

Prophet clan did not support Kerrick's illegitimate children being entitled to the estate.

Luckily for the newbies Nine didn't give a fuck, she alone was in charge, especially after she verified their bloodline. Besides, their history mirrored hers, dark and extremely secretive and she always rooted for the underdogs.

Many years ago Kerrick, always a man of great appetite, had an affair with Bridget Danker. A beautiful black woman with skin so light she could pass for white.

Their first child, Lisa, Bridget hid from Kerrick. But unlike his mistress Fran, surprisingly Bridget never attempted to reach out to his wife and so he allowed her the additional honor of baring him more children. But there was one condition, that when they were older that she explained to them how important it was to keep their bloodline pure.

At first Bridget was disgusted but Kerrick was a great speaker who explained that his lineage came from the kings and queens of Africa. In his delusion, he talked about how intelligent his older children were and how even in Roman times incest was accepted.

After awhile she was sold and when her children were born she allowed Kerrick to push the same rigid beliefs into their minds as he did the others. Before long Bridget gave birth to triplets Wagner, Porter and Jeremy, each with skin as yellow as lemons who although later were flawed.

For instance one of Wagner's eyes were cocked due to wearing a pair of prescription glasses when he didn't need them as a kid. And then there was Porter who kept his top lip pulled down because his teeth were crumbled due to improper dental care. Finally there was Jeremy, who lost his arm when his brothers and sister busted into an abandoned house where his mother, Bridget, was being gang raped after she left the home during a psychotic episode. All the assailants got away but one of them chopped off Jeremy's arm for the trouble.

Thinking on their feet, and upon hearing news that Kerrick was dead, they reached out to Nine who brought them under her realm and paid for Porter's teeth, Jeremy's expensive prosthetic arm and even looked for better care for Wagner's eye, although she'd been unsuccessful. And now they sat at the table, millionaires in their own right, by way of Nine Prophet.

While everyone laughed and had a good time Samantha who had one glass of wine too many asked, "So Nine, where's Leaf? He don't ever be around no more."

It was as if a record was scratched and the room grew quiet.

Nine stopped walking and looked down at her. "Do you see him?"

"No," Samantha cleared her throat.

"Then don't waste your voice on stupid inquiries." It was obvious that Samantha's question angered Nine but no one knew why. Irritated, Nine took a seat and said, "Now bring me news of the rest."

Noel scratched his cropped curly hair and looked at Nine and then Samantha and Bethany, his sisters. Both of them elected to pull their thick black hair in buns for the evening, jewels covered in ice aligning their necks.

Clearing his throat he said, "Our parents...are...asking for mercy again." He paused. "And I know they tried to have the estate taken away from you and it could've ruined your life but...well...I'm just bringing you their requests."

Nine placed both of her hands on the table, palms flat as she glared at him. "And you come to me about this because?"

"Well, we were hoping you could kick them a little something because they spent every dollar they got," Samantha said softly. "Mama blew through all the savings—"

"They tried to have me pushed out!" Nine yelled. "Plotted with you and everything, Noel."

"But I told you what I knew." He reminded her. "Remember? I chose you."

"Which is why you're able to sit at this table today." She said looking at him square in the eyes. "But Blake and Victory are dead to me and the other traitor too."

Noel, Samantha and Bethany looked at one another. "Do you mean Marina?" Bethany asked softly. "Because I heard she's in rehab, Nine. She may have been using drugs when she tried to take you down but—"

"Whether she is or not is of no consequence to me. I gave them all chances and each stabbed me in the back and as a result I have moved on." She paused. "Now if you want to give them your funds

I can have my attorney redirect your payments and—"

As if on a chorus they all yelled, "NO!"

"I figured as much." She grinned.

Completely silent, the triplets Wagner, Porter and Jeremy looked at each other. They took the cold lesson their brothers and sisters endured to heart, knowing they could be cut off too if they chose to betray her.

"Now, let's talk about our holiday party." Nine clapped her hands together. "Is everything going as planned?"

Bridget smiled and scooted closer to the table to flip open the manila folder sitting on top of it. Over the years Bridget had done wonders to make things easier for Nine by stepping in whenever she could. From massaging Nine's swollen feet when they ached, to directing the household staff and caring for the next generation of Prophets, the children, Bridget had done it all and Nine considered her invaluable.

"So far everything seems to be flowing well." Bridget said. "The caterers are all set and—"

When Nine's phone rang she picked it up and looked at the screen. "I have to get this. Please continue to discuss everything and we'll go from there." She raised an empty bottle of wine. "Go to the cellar and grab another bottle of Francesca and bring it to the table, Lisa." She placed it down. "We need to keep the party going." Although she didn't partake as much as the others, she did reserve the right to have a glass a night after reading a doctor's magazine stating that it was okay during pregnancy. And as stressed as she'd been lately she was looking for an excuse.

Nine scooted back from the table and Jeremy who had one arm and a prosthetic limb quickly jumped up and helped Nine to her feet. She smiled at him for the courtesy. "Thank you."

He winked. "My pleasure."

Noel glared feeling he was sucking up too much while Bridget on the other hand grinned proudly. He was her favorite child and she definitely wanted him to stay in favor with their financier.

"Don't worry," Noel whispered to his sister Bethany who was also his lover. "They won't last for long."

She looked at Jeremy who was helping Nine and nodded her head in agreement.

Stepping in the corner Nine took the call. "Leaf. Where...where are you?"

LEAF

Leaf sat in the parking lot of a strip club with a bottle of vodka in his hand as he spoke to his wife. His eyes were red and the designer blue jeans he was wearing were soiled with the vomit from earlier when his body got mad at him and purged the hours of liquor he swallowed along with the little food he consumed that day.

He told her he was handling business for their wine brand but the truth was he didn't give a fuck about the company either which way. Besides, the bottlers handled the production and all he did was show up, sign a check every now and again and pretend to be listening in the endless meetings they scheduled.

At the end of the day he was bored and only wanted to be with his wife. "I'm going to be late," Leaf said sipping vodka.

"Leaf, again?"

He guzzled some more. “Does it matter?” He wiped his mouth with the back of his hand.

She took a deep breath. “What is wrong with you?”

“So now your memory is trash?” He paused. “I tell you constantly how I feel and…you know what…it doesn’t matter.”

Nine took a deep breath. “They are my blood and my responsibility. I can’t put my family out on the streets.”

“Just ‘cause they’re blood doesn’t mean they’ll bleed for you.”

Silence.

“I wish you could see how important it is to have family around, especially with us having our first healthy child. We need to accept all the help we can get,” She paused. “I didn’t get a chance to do any of this when I was growing up and now we have an opportunity to build a strong foundation for our baby and—”

“So I’m not enough?”

“I never said that.”

“I gotta go.”

“Leaf, I—”

He ended the call and flung the iPhone in the passenger seat of his silver Aston Martin. He was done talking to her. Nine Prophet always did what Nine Prophet wanted and no one had yet succeeded in getting her to change her mind.

Leaf was sick with it all. Niggas were everywhere. The cousins, the people in and out of the mansion and most importantly Antonius, her most precious soldier, had Leaf feeling like he had no place at her side and he was growing hateful as a result.

Leaf put his car into drive. He was about to pull away when directly to his right, within a pile of bushes he noticed something moving. Leaning closer he saw a dog was attempting to hide itself.

"What the fuck you doing, lil nigga?" He parked, opened the door and walked toward it. There in the brush sat a chocolate Labrador growling softly when he moved closer. Drunk and needing to feel something, Leaf pursued the animal anyway.

CHAPTER TWO

ANTONIUS

"Yes, for a score of kingdoms you should wrangle, and I would call it fair play."

- William Shakespeare

Antonius sat on a small stool across from Alice who had been locked in Nine's mansion for almost two years. Sunrays from a small window on the right, the only indicator of night and day, shined into her cell, causing shade lines on her face.

Alice scratched the old scars on her cheek, compliments of the revenge torture that Nine subjected her to for sixteen weeks, some years back after she abused Nine first. But upon discovering that even after Nine showed Alice mercy by letting her live that she still plotted to take the Prophet estate from her, Nine subjected her to a new kind of torture.

Life in a dark cell.

Away from attention and the limelight.

Despite it all, she was still alluring. Her long hair tamed in two messy French braids that ran down the middle of her back and the white soiled nightgown that she wore failed to make her ugly.

"You don't have to do this you know?" Alice said as she clutched at the bars and looked over at him.

"It's my job."

Antonius was beyond attractive and yet he didn't even know it. His skin was espresso and without a flaw. His baldhead was smooth and his black goatee seemed to set off his mystical features. Wearing only a white t-shirt that showcased his bulging muscles along with designer blue jeans and a black leather gun belt, he looked ready to eat and ready for war at the same damn time.

She shook her head. "Antonius, I heard her telling you to just peek in on me months ago. And to not talk to me. But you never seem to leave. Why is that?"

He took a deep breath. "I go where I want."

"That is clear. I just wished you could at least—"

"I can't." He exhaled. "So don't ask me."

She looked away, up at the small window. "How do you know what I was about to say?"

"Because I know."

Alice took a deep breath. "I have been locked up for almost two years. Never seeing the light of day, outside of the window you built for me a few months back. Please, free me. Let me run away and I promise to never return."

"The window I built is because I detected your sadness. Although I know your grief is Nine's purpose I did so anyway and you should be grateful."

She laughed softly. "Should I be?" She squeezed the bars tightly and pushed half of her face through the slats. "Let me out, Antonius. Please. I can tell in your eyes that you are a kind person. This isn't right. And you know it."

"I heard a lot wasn't right when you did what you did to Nine too." He glared. "The beatings. Remember?"

"But I'm changed! Can't you see?"

Antonius looked away. "I'm not here for that."

"Look at me," she demanded.

He didn't.

"Fucking look at my face!"

Slowly he turned his head toward the bars and looked at her expression. "Maybe you are changed." He stood up and walked toward her. "But what kind of mind could treat Nine the way you did in the first place? How do I know that these bars aren't preventing you from doing more?"

She took a deep breath. "I am a child born to Marina and Joshua Saint." She walked away from the bars and sat on the stool in her cell. "My mother was an addict and evil. And I may have been many things but I wasn't born that way, Antonius. I only acted out on what I knew and I will forever be sorry for my actions. But...this...is wrong. Everyday I feel myself dying inside...and I can't take much more."

"Nine was locked up in this basement for over fifteen years."

"More than that." She corrected him.

"And yet you fall apart at two," He glared.

She shook her head and started crying. The type of cry that pulled from the heart and called out to all those within ear distance. "You are right. I deserve everything I am getting." She sniffled.

Feeling guilty he brought on her agony; he walked away and leaned against the wall across from the cell. What was this woman doing to him? "To answer your earlier question, I'm here because...well...I want to see if it's possible for you to be changed," he whispered.

She looked up, wiped her tears and walked to the bars, hands gripped tightly on them, knuckles whitening. "Really?"

"I can't make any promises, Alice. I wouldn't if I could because it's still not my say." He took a deep breath. "But if you are changed maybe I can talk to Nine."

"You would do that for me?"

"I feel your despair and—"

"What's going on in here?" Lisa asked walking into the door, holding two bottles of wine under her arms. "And who is...who is she, Antonius?" Although Alice looked like the person at the meeting who made a mistake of trying to steal the estate years ago, Alice had lost so much weight along with her millionaire shine that she could no longer confirm her identity.

Wearing a long black gown with large cascades of black curled hair running down her shoulders and back she stood stunned at the woman in the cell.

Antonius rushed over to the door, pushed her back and slammed it behind himself as he walked out. He forgot Nine's cardinal rule to always lock the door leading to Alice's cell and now there was a witness.

Having been the sole responsibility for Alice for years, he had gotten too comfortable with nobody coming downstairs. Not even Nine visited in awhile because the arguments she got into with Alice had her feeling extreme rage. And since she was pregnant she elected to protect her peace and her baby's wellbeing.

"Who...who is that person?" Lisa asked looking up at him but pointing at the door. Lisa knew the cellar was nowhere near that room but for almost two years she had been fascinated by its existence, making every attempt to enter and find out what they were hiding. And now she succeeded. "Is that...Alice?"

"You aren't supposed to be here." He glared. "What are you doing down here anyway?"

"I was getting wine out of the cellar." She looked at the closed door again.

"And the cellar is on the other side of this house." He pointed behind her.

"I know but...I..."

"Got nosey," he said, his nostrils flaring.

She nodded. "I'm sorry."

Frustrated he took a few steps away and came back quickly. Taking a deep breath he wiped his hand down his face and sighed. "Listen, you can't tell anyone about what you saw in there. Especially not—"

Suddenly his cell phone rung and he put up his finger at Lisa who used the moment to run away. "Hello..." *Fuck*, he said under his breath after watching her leave without injecting the fear of God into her first. "Who is this?"

"Antonius, you have to come now," a frantic voice pled on the other end of the line.

"What's going on?"

"It's Nine. She's in trouble."

Antonius dropped his phone and dipped upstairs.

NINE

Nine's labor was a success.

Finally.

The first baby ended in miscarriage due to too close genes.

But this one was picture perfect.

And as she held her son in her hands and smiled down at him she oozed with gratitude. He cooed softly but otherwise held a smile on his face as he looked up at his mother. A baby born of incest, he surprisingly was one hundred percent healthy.

With him in her arms she wondered how it was possible for a mother to not feel the extreme love she felt in that moment. She wondered why her own mother treated her as an abomination, not fit to be loved or cherished. Although she'd never tell another soul, almost everyday she longed for Kelly's love.

Antonius, standing at her side smiled down at her. "Wow, he's perfect." He ran his finger alongside the baby's yellow face.

She looked up at him. "Thank you so much for being there for me. I don't know where—"

"You're my everything, Nine. Where else would I be?" His words came out like that of a man in love and not that of a man in service to a woman who was his boss. "I'm sorry, I didn't mean it that way."

"You don't have to lie to me. I know how you feel."

He smiled but looked away. “And still it’s wrong. You belong to Leaf.”

“Forever and for always.” She confirmed although hurt he wasn’t available to take the call when she went into labor. “He saved me from myself but it doesn’t mean that I am not fond of you. You know that don’t you?”

Silence.

“I didn’t know.” He exhaled. “Until now.”

She took a deep breath and looked down at her baby again. “How can he be so perfect and be mine? After all of the things I’ve done and all the people I hurt, God still saw fit to endow me with so much beauty.”

“You deserve this.”

“I can’t say that is true.” She gazed up at him again and examined how attractive he was. He looked good enough to eat. “You know what, Antonius, after all this time I’m surprised I still have your eye.”

“Meaning?”

“You are a very handsome and wealthy man since you’ve been under my employ. Yet there isn’t anyone you think about being with other than me?”

"It sounds like you trying to get rid of me." He laughed once.

"Never leave me."

Suddenly a nurse entered and took the baby for tests and for rest for Nine. Nine sighed deeply.

"Is there anything I can do for you, Nine?" Antonius asked touching her face.

"Nah, but you can do something for me, bruh," Leaf said entering the room bringing with him the rage of a jealous man and the funk of a drunk. "You can get the fuck outta here. Can you handle that?"

Antonius snatched his hand off Nine's face and cleared his throat. "Hey, Leaf. I was just...uh...checking on Nine."

"That's all you got to say to me?" Leaf paused. "I mean you touching my wife, nigga. The least you could do is give me more than that."

"It wasn't like that," Antonius said. "I was just—"

"Fuck up out my face, nigga." Leaf roared waving the air. "Before I unleash in this bitch."

"Leaf!" Nine yelled.

"Now!" Leaf continued, eyes trained on Antonius.

Antonius nodded and looked down at Nine. "I'll see you at the house."

"Yeah, you do that." Leaf said, teeth clenched.

Antonius walked passed him and out the door.

"On my pulsing veins I will see him hit dirt, believe that," Leaf said.

"You didn't have to be so cruel."

"You mean I don't have to stand by and watch my wife fall in love with another nigga? Before my eyes?" Leaf walked up to the bed. "What is up with you and that dude?" He ran his hand down his face. "Why you gotta keep some *'Just In Case Dick'* around? Huh?"

"I said it before and I'll say it again, nothing is going on with us. He just happens to be a good friend and—"

"I want him out the house."

"Leaf, I—"

"Nah, fuck that, I want them all out." He moved closer. "I mean, why can't it just be you and I? Why the crowd all the time?"

"We have a home with more rooms than we can live in. Julius, Denarius and Kerrick II can only live in three and they are children. Why can't we share our wealth with our family?"

They certainly had some kids up in that bitch.

Julius was four years old and actually her nephew that she raised after killing her sister Paige when she tried to kill her first. Denarius was the son of Galileo whom she also had to kill for his betrayal while electing to raise his son when Shawna, his mother, died in a car accident. And finally there was Kerrick II, her toddler cousin. He was also the child of Wagner and Lisa, sister and brother.

"I want to be with just you, Julius and our son." He took a deep breath. "All others don't matter to me because just like you have been betrayed before for money, you will be betrayed again for the same thing."

"You come here with so much rage in your heart, Leaf. And yet you didn't even ask about your son."

He sighed. "I'm sorry. What did you name him?"

"I didn't give him a name. I wanted you here for that part."

"Then he will be called Magnus Prophet." Leaf said proudly.

Nine smiled. "I like that. A lot."

"Do you?" He looked at her, grabbed a miniature vodka bottle from his pocket and swallowed half of it. "Well that's good or whatever."

Her eyes widened. "Leaf, you can't drink here!"

"Well I guess I better leave then." He smiled and walked toward the door.

"Leaf!" She continued. "I'm talking to you!" He walked out. "What about your son?"

NINE

After putting Magnus to sleep and helping Bridget put up life size dolls scattered around the house that Kerrick II and Julius loved to play with, Nine walked to the room Francesca, her grandfather's secret lover and the woman Nine truly loved, stayed inside when she was alive. It was not much larger than a walk-in closet within the basement and yet there Nine often felt at home.

Opening the closet, Nine ran her fingers over the tattered clothing Fran used to wear. When she happened upon a nun's habit she smiled. Before she died Fran told her of all the places she'd gone in an effort to escape Kerrick's obsessive and abusive affections toward her. What she wouldn't give for a crazy kind of love from Leaf.

Holding the habit to her face she inhaled. "Fran, my life is coming down around me. Please, if you are still watching over me, lend me your hand. I need a mother's love."

CHAPTER THREE

KELLY & ISABEL PROPHET

"If he could right himself with quarreling, some of us would lie low."

- William Shakespeare

Seated in the back of a stretch Mercedes limousine, Kelly and Isabel Prophet cruised down the street on the way to Aristocrat Hills. After many years in an institution, Kelly was looking forward to returning to the home she grew up in to be one again with her father's presence. How she missed him, even obsessing over the days when she could live next to his spirit.

Once a disappointment by never being able to give Kerrick a grandchild he was proud of with her brother Avery, she ignored each of her children. First there was Paige and Lydia, Irish twins, who were fat and dirty since she refused to care for them, electing to feed them too much instead of love them. After some time came Nine, the ninth grandchild whose skin was chocolate causing her to be considered as an abomination for which she was later tortured.

Kelly blamed the world for her stint in the institution courtesy of Kerrick who had her committed before he died to prevent her from drawing attention to the Prophet clan and their ways. Believing that if she had not been taken then the love of her life, her brother Avery would not have put a gun to his head and blew his brains out in front of Nine, she longed for revenge.

Time may have passed but hate still swam in Kelly's heart. Her face was now gaunt and her hair silver from anger and worry. "Finally," Kelly said to no one in particular.

Isabel didn't bother to look at her aunt. Besides, they shared rooms next to each other in the mental institution and she'd had enough of her rambling for a lifetime.

Unlike Kelly, Isabel's mental instability came as a result of being abused sexually by her father and other men who he sold her too. Still beautiful, soft curls sprouted from the edges of the long ponytail she had running down her back.

"Tell me Isabel, are you excited?"

Not wanting to humor her aunt she elected to shrug instead. Besides, she didn't know what the fool was talking about.

"Well you should be." Kelly eyed the luxurious vehicle, as if seeing it for the first time. "This is the turning point of your life." She ran her hands along the black leather seats. "Of our lives."

"How?" Isabel looked at her strangely.

"I have a chance to allow Nine back into my good graces."

"Back into *your* good graces?" She paused. "She is your daughter. Why should it be a problem?"

"It won't you pretty fool," Kelly said. "It won't at all." Kelly closed her eyes and suddenly urine flowed out of her body and into the leather seats. She was essentially marking her territory.

Seeing this Isabel jumped up and sat across from her. "What is wrong with you?"

"Not one single thing," Kelly laughed heavily.

LEAF

Leaf watched the pregnant dog he rescued drink water after just eating in the basement of the mansion. Although he was rewarded by a bite to his hand for his efforts, he still managed to place the animal inside of his car and drive her to the house. Sitting in a white plastic chair with a six-pack shy of two, he plucked one open and took a large gulp.

The dog, now full, wobbled over to the floor bed and flopped down. Barely able to hold her own weight, she spent most days stretched out in the open waiting to give birth. The only difference is now she had him to protect her.

Suddenly the door opened and Nine walked into the room. Wearing jeans and a white wife beater, which caressed her curves, she was already starting to regain her figure. "There you are."

He sipped his beer. "Been here all night."

"I know although I don't understand why." He took another sip of beer, ignoring her comment. "Well I just put the baby to sleep." She sighed. "The boys are loving him already and—"

"The mental institution called, Nine." He continued to focus on the animal. "I know what you've done. You don't have to come down here with all the fake shit."

"Leaf, I'm sorry but I—"

"Why bother?" He turned his head to look at her. "Huh? Why bother to tell me anything when it's obvious you gonna do what you want anyway?"

"It's my mother and cousin," she whispered.

"No! What it is, is that you have the hero syndrome!" He yelled. "Why would you let into our home a woman who hated you and kept you under this house? A mother who allowed you to be beaten like a dog? And a cousin who almost killed me?"

"What do you want me to do?"

"Does it matter, Nine?" He roared. "Does any of it matter?"

The dog suddenly growled at Nine and she noticed. "It'll only be for a week, Leaf. Until I find them someplace else to stay."

"Who you fooling?" He drunk the rest of the beer and tossed the can across the room. It almost hit her foot.

"No one."

"Good, 'cause you and I both know that ain't happening. You very rarely allow your pet projects to go. Don't see how this will be any different." He let loose another beer from the pack and drunk it all.

Nine took a deep breath. "I wish you would trust me."

"Get out, Nine. I'm sick of you."

KELLY

Isabel and Kelly walked through the door of the mansion while the rest of the household stood behind Nine, each doing their best to get a look at the woman responsible for the most powerful woman they know being born.

Noel and Bethany who had been spending more time on the estate to make sure the illegitimates didn't get more money than them were also present. Plus they wanted to see their crazy sister Isabel after so many years.

"She way lighter than Nine," Lisa whispered to Wagner, her brother and also her boyfriend while holding Kerrick II in her arms.

He gave her a serious look, silencing her immediately.

Nine on the other hand was as stiff as a statue. There was still so much hate in her heart for the way Kelly treated her as a child and she didn't know how to handle it. On the inside small voices screamed that Kelly should not be allowed in the home Nine's grandfather, and Kelly's father, gifted to Nine. But the other part of her wanted desperately to have the love of a mother.

Then there was Isabel. Although she was originally angry, with time and medication she started to warm to Nine. But it was Kelly who Nine had high hopes about.

Kelly smiled and walked up to Nine slowly. Standing in front of her she placed cool hands on the sides of Nine's face. "Thank you."

Nine backed out of her mother's embrace, remembering the ugly things she would scream at her when she was younger. During the visits at the mental institution they never touched and Kelly's embrace felt, well, cold. "Thank me for what?"

"For letting me stay here," Kelly smiled. "In your home. Where I can be close to father's presence."

Nine took a deep breath. “This is only temporary.”

“And it doesn’t matter,” Kelly said passionately. “I’ll take whatever time I can get as long as I can be with you.”

Nine looked away.

Needing a breather from her mother she walked up to Isabel who hugged Nine tightly. “Hello cousin.” Nine said with a wide smile. “I’m glad you’re here.”

Isabel hugged her again. “You kept your word.”

“I told you I would. Didn’t you believe me?”

She shrugged, and walked toward each new face as if they were wax sculptures in a museum. She remembered some of them but time fogged her memory. “Yes, but Prophets have a history of not doing what they say.” She paused and turned to look at Nine again. “And I take by the many yellow faces surrounding me, you have found yourself even more.”

Nine laughed heartedly. “You’re right about that.”

“Hello, sister,” Noel said to Isabel.

“Brother.” She replied.

After Nine reintroduced Kelly and Isabel to Kerrick's illegitimate children, they retired to the dining room where a large meal lay before them. Everyone took their place at the table with a capacity to feed many.

While eating, Kelly, who sat next to Nine, looked toward the far end of the table. "Where is Leaf?"

Nine looked down and took a deep breath. "Let's just say we are family and family doesn't always see eye to eye. And so is the case for me and my husband."

Nine stood up, holding a glass of Francesca wine in her hand. Kelly noticed the bottle and frowned upon seeing the woman's name and Isabel, who saw all, caught her hateful aunt's gaze.

"Let us make a toast. To the Prophet clan."

"To the Prophet clan!" Everyone cheered before the room grew eerily silent.

Taking an even larger breath before looking at the chair where her husband was not present, Nine clapped her hands once and said, "Let us drink and be merry!"

LEAF

The morning rays came through the window above as Leaf stood in front of his dog that was giving birth. Not knowing what to do, he paced briskly as if he were losing his mind. Suddenly he felt stupid as fuck for bringing the animal into his home in the first place. He wasn't no fucking doctor.

What was he thinking?

Antonius, on his way to the section of the house Alice was kept, stopped when he saw Leaf through the open doorway. "Everything cool?" Antonius asked.

The moment Leaf heard his voice he grew irritated. "Your precious *boss* ain't down here. Keep it moving, my nigga."

"I know, man. I was just—"

"THEN WHAT THE FUCK YOU WANT?"

Antonius took a deep breath and walked further into the room anyway. "Listen, I used to breed pits. I know how to do this if you want help. If you don't I can get with that too."

"Well what if...what if I..."

The dog moaned and Leaf grew more agitated.

"Let me help, man." He paused. "You can go back to hating me later."

Leaf looked at the dog and back at Antonius. "What you need?"

"A box, scissors, clean towels, one of them bulb syringes in the kitchen, floss and some gloves." Antonius pushed back the sleeves to the black Gucci cashmere sweater he was wearing.

"Aight...," Leaf paused. "I'll be right back."

"Bring a space heater too!"

Antonius tended to the dog until Leaf came back by softly stroking its head. When Leaf brought the items he knew it was time to get to work. First Antonius cut the box open and placed them around the corner of a section of wall. Then he placed towels on the floor neatly."

"How long this supposed to take?" Leaf asked as Antonius slid gloves on.

"She's already in labor so about two hours." Antonius looked at him once more. "Why you doing this, man? Breeding dogs and shit? This seems off the grid for your personality."

"You helping or judging?"

Antonius shook his head and lifted the dog and put him in the corner on the towels. After some time the dog was ready to give birth. The animal lifted its tail and one by one puppies were pushed out into the world.

Once they came the mother would lick at the birthing sac so the puppies were free from the soft material surrounding them. Two of the puppies couldn't get free so Antonius lifted each, tore open the sack carefully and syringed their mouths when they were choking. He also severed the umbilical cords with scissors.

Leaf, feeling worthless once again that he paled in comparison to the great Antonius, stood in the corner glaring at him for touching his bitch. He didn't like him then and he definitely didn't like him now.

Three hours later five puppies were born and Leaf was unusually excited, more excited than he had been for the birth of his son.

"What now?" Leaf asked gritting his teeth.

Antonius sighed. "Um...food and water for the mother and just leave them alone. She needs to nurse and bond with them so you don't want to touch them too much." Antonius took the gloves off and tossed them in the trash. "Anything else?"

Leaf rolled his eyes. *I hate this nigga.* He thought to himself.

"I guess I won't even get a thank you huh?"

Silence.

Antonius sighed. "No matter what you want to believe, I'm not the enemy. Maybe one day you'll realize that." He looked at the animals again. "Well, let me go. You should be good from here."

Leaf's gaze remained on the dogs. "What?"

It was obvious to Antonius in that moment that Leaf had gone mad, and he wondered how much worse things would get from there.

ANTONIUS

A WEEK LATER

Alice stood up in her cell when Antonius walked in holding a small box in one hand and a plastic bag in the other. He sat the items on a chair by the door, locked it and then picked them up walking toward her. First he handed her the bag through the bars.

Once in her hand, she placed it against her nose. “This doesn’t smell like the rice and peas Nine normally makes that you give me.” She looked at him. “What is it?”

He walked away, scooted a chair closer to the bars while still holding the box in his lap. “Nothing.”

She sat on the bin in the cell and tore into the bag. Her eyes lit up when she saw fried chicken and fries inside. Gobbling the food, almost without breathing she was transported to Foodie Heaven. Each bite was savory and had her eyes rolling toward the back of her head. With a mouth full she said, “Wow...Antonius, you’re my favorite.”

He chuckled. “For now.”

“Why you say that?” He stood up and moved the box toward the bars and inside was a beautiful black lab puppy a week old. He had developed a grey stripe down the top of his head and was adorable. “Oh, my god, Antonius! Is she...is she mine?” Placing the food on the bed she said, “Can I hold her?”

“She’s yours...well, I’m working it out anyway.” He paused. “But you can’t hold her yet because it's too early. I'm not supposed to even have her."

Alice looked down at the puppy and large tears rolled down her cheeks. The innocence of the animal in that moment gave her hope for the future. "It's the most beautiful thing I've—" Not able to take anymore she tossed herself on the bed and wept.

Seeing her pain Antonius picked up the puppy and placed it gently back in the box. Next he dug into his pocket and pulled out the key to the cell. Before opening the door he looked at the gold key hard. Going inside, something he'd never done would be the end of his loyalty to Nine and he wasn't sure if he was willing to take the risk. Still, something was happening between him and Alice and he wanted to scratch that itch, even if it led nowhere.

In those moments his mind reminded him constantly of the torture Nine endured under Alice's watch, based on Nine's accounts of course. Yes. Alice's rep was long and hard but the woman in front of him seemed different, at least that's what he wanted to believe.

"Alice, I..."

"Just go, please."

"Alice—"

"Just go!" She yelled wiping tears off her scarred face roughly.

"I'm not leaving you like this."

"Why not?" She paused. "Huh? Because its obvious you think I'm a monster. I can see it in your eyes."

"If I truly believe that then why am I here?"

"No, if you truly believed that why are you still on the other side when you have the key to enter?" She said softly pointing at it in his palm. "Antonius, I have not been held at all in well over a year. Please, I'm begging you to hold me. I'm begging you to touch me."

Antonius placed the key in the lock, turned and looked down. Nine's face suddenly came into his mind. There was something about Alice that called him but his heart still belonged to Nine even if he could never have her as he wanted.

Instead of going inside he locked the door. "I'm sorry." He picked the box up and dropped the key back into his pocket. "But I can't do this."

Alice leapt up and grabbed the bars. "Antonius, don't leave me!"

NINE

Nine stood in front of the mirror looking at her curvaceous body. The plan was to seduce Leaf and bring him back to her bed, some place he hadn't been since Kelly and Isabel arrived.

She understood his anger. And as far as her heart could tell she had no intentions on letting them stay. The plan was to buy a small house for them away from the mansion. But somewhere deep inside she also harbored the desire for them to remain, living happily ever after as if that were ever a thing for Prophets.

Fingering her short curly hair in the mirror, she was about to walk downstairs to the basement where she knew Leaf was when Kelly walked into the room. Her hair died black while she once again looked like a millionaire. "Wow, you're beautiful." She stood behind Nine and looked at her skin tone, shades away from her own.

"Thank you, mother."

Kelly placed her hands on Nine's shoulders. "I'm sorry, Nine."

Nine's belly bubbled. She wanted to hear those words all of her life and now she had. "For...for...what?"

"I was jealous. I was, I was jealous of the relationship you had with my father and it caused me to see you different from who you really are. Plus father had some preferences that had me wanting to create the perfect child to please him without realizing I already had it with you."

"Momma, I—" Nine turned around and Kelly touched her face again. She closed her eyes as if she were a child, cherishing the soft touch of her mother. Her stomach bubbled again and her knees felt weak.

"I'm sorry," Kelly said gently. "I'm so sorry and I only hope that with time you could forgive me." She hugged Nine strongly and Nine wept in her arms.

"Momma, I...I..." She was so overcome with emotion that she could barely talk. These were the words she never thought she would hear and now they were pouring out of Kelly in ways Nine could not comprehend.

"And when I leave I hope that you and I can still build on our relationship. I hope that I can learn to be the mother you wanted and needed as a child." Kelly kissed her once more and Nine dropped to her knees and cried harder.

A lifetime of emotion pouring out of her pores.

"Why now, mama?" Nine looked up at her. "Why, why in this moment?"

"Because I'm dying, Nine." She helped Nine up and they both sat on the edge of the bed. "I have cancer of the breasts and the doctors don't think I'll live long."

"But...I...I thought you were healthy." She wiped her tears away.

"No, I'm not. And I asked them to keep that part away from you because I didn't want you letting me stay here out of pity. I genuinely wanted to find out if we could repair our relationship."

"Mama, I...I can't let you leave." Nine sniffled. "You aren't well. Let me talk to Leaf and see what I can do."

"No, Nine." Kelly walked toward the window overlooking the vineyards for effect. "I don't think that would be right and I don't think my nephew would like it."

"But I need you to get well. Let me talk to him."

Kelly turned around. "Are you sure, my precious daughter?"

"I'm positive, mama." She placed her hand on her heart. "I'll deal with Leaf. We may fight but he really is a good man and he loves me."

"Honey, I don't know if you see things the way we do but it's obvious that there's trouble in paradise." Kelly walked toward her. "Leaf has made it known that he doesn't want me, Isabel and the rest of the clan here. Are you sure letting us stay will be good for your relationship? The last thing I want to do is cause you problems."

Nine took a deep breath. "Leaf has seen a lot of things. He's seen me at my worst and I think he's afraid of me losing stability. But trust me, he will come around."

"I understand." Kelly said after taking a deep breath. "And what of Isabel? Maybe you should send her away at least. Since she's the one who almost stabbed him."

"Isabel will be Isabel." Nine sighed. "I do know I'm not comfortable with her being out on her own without you. Originally the plan was to buy you both a house but now...well now things are changed. If you are staying she must too."

Kelly sighed not wanting that crazy bitch to be roped up with her. "I will take your judgment. But I do want you to know that I'm against it because a good man is a troublesome thing to find. And you have that right now like I had with my brother, your father."

Nine nodded.

"Well, let me go check on my grandson. It's odd; I can't believe how good Bridget is with the kids. Daddy may have slept with her over momma's head but he picked a good one didn't he?" She smiled. "And I heard she's even started homeschooling the boys."

"Yes, she came to me with the idea earlier and since our lifestyle causes so many problems in public I think it will be for the best."

"I agree. She is certainly precious." Kelly walked over to Nine and kissed her on the forehead. "I'll be back later."

Having gotten what she wanted, Kelly walked out with a glare that was hidden from Nine. The last thing she wanted was to repair a relationship with her worthless black ass daughter. She wanted power. Total power. And now she was going to put her plan into action. But to do that she would first have to convince Nine to let her stay and without asking directly and lying her face off she succeeded.

"Nine, soon what's yours will be mine," Kelly whispered to herself. "As it should have always been."

CHAPTER FOUR

NINE

"Nay, and I tell you that, I'll never look you in the face again."

- William Shakespeare

Nine sat across from Leaf for a candle light dinner. The meal consisted of blue cheese steak, twice baked mini potatoes and chocolate mousse. When the food was served and they ate, all in silence of course, Nine looked over at him. "I love you."

"I know." He scratched his thick curly hair and grabbed a toothpick out of the sterling silver holder for his teeth.

She took a deep breath, trying to find the right words to reach his soul. "Leaf, if you tap out on me I don't know what I'm going to do. So much of the woman I am today has everything to do with you being there for me." She touched her heart. "And if you go away mentally I, I'm afraid of what I may become."

"Then how do we solve it?" He placed his fork down and leaned back in his seat, eyes peering into her soul. “I’m the nigga you chose to be at your side and yet I can’t get you to respect me.”

“That’s not true.”

“You know what, I’m not doing this.” He tossed the toothpick down and wiped the corner of his mouth with the white linen napkin.

“Wait!” She yelled.

Fearing he was about to leave, Nine stood up, raised the gold slinky dress she was wearing and eased on the table, pushing the food aside gently as she made her way to him. Now sitting in front of him like a snack she raised her dress and looked down at him.

As mad as he was when it came to Nine’s fuck game he was no match. Eyes on his beautiful wife’s flesh, the color of strong espresso coffee, he released his stiff penis stood up and pulled her closer. The moment he pushed into her pinkness her head flew back, exposing her diamond studded neck.

Gripping her ass cheeks, he drilled harder and harder before he got so rough it began to hurt. Filled with ecstasy and pain at the same time, Nine could see the rage in his eyes and it both excited and worried her. If he no longer cherished her who was she?

Biting down on his bottom lip, he continued to slam into her body until he felt himself ready to explode. "I love you, Leaf. Don't...don't leave me."

"Shut up," he said as he continued to pound. When he could take no more of the anger and pleasure he was feeling, instead of planting his seed inside of her he ejaculated on her Versace dress, treating her like a slut. "The pussy ain't never been a problem," he said as he placed his dick back into his pants. "Your attitude is."

Enraged she slapped him for his disrespect and he laughed before walking away. Neither knowing that Antonius stood in the corner, observing it all.

ISABEL

Sitting in Fran's room, a place she found comfort because the small dark place reminded her of the mental institution, Isabel focused on the objects she saw that she was certain weren't there. People dressed in loud colors of red, orange and blue were laughing and pointing their long fingers her way.

Being able to control her mental episodes had never been a problem before she was locked up. But after being placed in the institution she realized she couldn't let others know that at the end of the day she was very much still crazy.

When the door opened Porter walked into the room. Smiling at her, he sat on the edge of the bed and stared at her for three minutes before saying anything.

"So you're a nun now?" He said pointing at the habit she was wearing.

"It keeps the demons away." She paused. "Which is why I don't understand why you're here."

He smiled, his new perfect white teeth gleaming. "I like you."

She ignored him.

"So, I don't know how this works but I'm going to jump out there. And shoot my shot. Have you selected a mate?" He paused. "I mean I know we supposed to stay together and—"

"I'm not interested in mating. I'm just twenty one years old—"

"You in the perfect child baring years."

She shook her head.

He laughed. "I'm serious. Isn't that the way of the Prophets? We breed amongst ourselves like daddy said?" He moved closer. "So how will you satisfy yourself? Sexually? If you don't choose?"

Wearing the habit, Isabel spread her legs, pushed her panties to the side and fingered her clit. She carried on for two minutes with Porter watching like she was Netflix, while stiffening in his pants. She didn't stop until she brought herself to ecstasy. "Like that." She pulled the habit down.

He laughed with everything he could. "Woman, if you think you're getting rid of me by acting this way you don't know me at all. I'll give you some time to come around. And in the meantime I'll be getting ready for you."

"You're a fool."

"And you will be mine," he continued.

She grabbed his shirt and wiped her cream on the bottom of it.

He brought it to his nose and inhaled. "Fresh. I love it." He stood up and looked down at her. "You and I." He nodded. "That's how I see this going down and I'm not gonna stop until I convince you of the same."

It wasn't until he walked out that Isabel grinned. She wasn't sure but somehow she believed he was right.

LEAF

Leaf sat in the backyard while watching his puppies run playfully around an area of the yard he fenced off. He was sipping a cold beer and thinking about his wife who he wished would be different. Remembering how she looked sitting on that table as he fucked her played in his mind on repeat and he felt himself about to be brought to orgasm even though he didn't touch himself.

And then Porter walked out and sat next to him. Ruining it all.

Pointing at the beer in the cooler he asked, "May I?"

"Nah." He looked at him harshly before focusing back on his animals. His dick quickly softened. "Ya'll be thinking ya'll got access to everything around here but I'm not Nine. This my beer, for me only!"

Porter nodded, figuring he would steal a little of his liquor later like he was accustomed. "You doing good with them." He nodded toward the labs. "The dogs."

Leaf sighed. "If you didn't already have everything you wanted I would grab my wallet. But that ain't the case since Nine made you a young millionaire. So stop fucking around and tell me what you really want."

"I want Izzy."

Leaf laughed heartedly.

"What's funny?" Porter asked.

"You picked the craziest bitch out the bunch to breed with." He shook his head. "I don't know why insane women seem so appealing to niggas. But be that as it may, you'd do well to stay the fuck away from that wacko."

"That ain't happening."

"Well you flirting with death," Leaf said firmly. "And I've warned you."

Porter scratched his nestle of curly hair that resembled Leaf's. "Do you love my niece? 'Cause it don't seem like ya'll feeling each other much these days."

"Look, new unc, do yourself a favor and bounce before I raise up."

Porter stood up. "You got it, nephew." He sighed. "I'll be out later to pick up behind the dogs. Nine fired the last landscaper because he was jacking off in front of mama and she got scared. At least that's what I heard anyway."

"Whatever," Leaf shrugged before grabbing another beer. "Just stay out my way. I ain't up for Prophet company these days. To tell you the truth I ain't up for shit."

JEREMY, WAGNER, LISA

Jeremy and Wagner lie on the bed looking at car magazines while Lisa counted money in her wallet. All three, including their brother Porter had cashed their checks of $8,000 a piece and were looking to live it up for the weekend. Before Nine came into the picture, Bridget and Kerrick's children mostly lived in poverty but now they were on cloud nine, no pun intended, and they were feeling themselves.

When they first arrived to Aristocrat they controlled the narrative by telling Nine that the family was so very close. Lisa and their pack even went as far as to say that Lisa and Wagner had gotten married and were hopelessly in love. The only truth they revealed was that their mother had mental episodes like the one that caused her to end up in an abandoned building naked and raped.

But the rest of their story was all lies.

The illegitimates were definitely troubled.

"Man, if she gave us a little more a month I could get this Benz," Jeremy said pointing at the magazine with his real finger, the other being a prosthetic.

"Right, then we could share," Wagner added, his eye cocked further to the side than normal.

Lisa put her money in her pocket. "Niggas always so greedy." She shook her head in disgust. "Nine be looking out for real. And if it wasn't for her, Wagner, our son would be out on the streets."

Wagner frowned and stood up. "So you acting like I ain't appreciating shit now?"

"Not saying that, but you should chill out with all this *I wish I had more* shit. I mean what you doing with the cash she's giving you now? It ain't like you dropping money on our baby's clothes. I be putting money up for Kerrick's college and shit like that because our stay here is not guaranteed."

"So do that then, but don't act like I'm not here for our kid." Wagner continued, one eye on her and the other only God knew where.

"Calm down, both of ya'll," Jeremy said getting up. "I understand what you saying, Lisa, but this money is rightfully ours. It was because of our vote that she was able to get at the whole trust from our other siblings. We are Kerrick's children not some niggas she took in off the street."

"And I know all that." Lisa continued. "But don't forget that when certain people tried to be greedy she kicked them all off the trust. Samantha and Bethany said their parents done ran through all them little coins and begging for a space back in Nine's graces as we speak. You trying to have that happen to us too?"

Wagner rolled his eye and sighed. "Man, she getting on my nerves."

Lisa waved the air. "Boy, just get out of my face."

Livid, Wagner smacked her to the floor while Jeremy rushed to close and lock the door. When she was down Wagner snatched her by the hair and put her on the bed, back against the mattress. Jeremy crawled on the bed so that her head was between his legs before slamming his hand over her mouth while Wagner punched her several times in the stomach, something they had done many times before coming to the mansion to relieve stress.

Before this moment Lisa felt comfortable that this awful part of her life was over because they were at Aristocrat Hills. But now she realized she was wrong. He didn't stop pounding her gut until she coughed up blood between Jeremy's fingers. And even then he got one more blow in.

"Let her go," Wagner said breathing heavily. When he did she rolled over and coughed more blood on the bed. "Don't think just because we here I'ma let you talk slick, bitch." He looked at his brother. "Let's bounce, twin."

Jeremy, always the follower, slid off the bed and walked out the door, leaving his sister alone.

CHAPTER FIVE

NINE

"So, again, good night. I must be cruel only to be kind."

- William Shakespeare

The fireplace crackled in Nine and Leaf's bedroom and when she rolled over in bed and placed her hand over Leaf's heart she was about to cry. He was asleep at first but when he felt her touch his eyes opened and he focused on the ceiling.

"Don't do it, Nine," he said softly. "I know I haven't said much but I'm begging you not to let them stay here. Especially your mother."

She removed her hand. "But I have to." She exhaled. "And I'm asking that you support me like always."

He turned his head toward her. "You mean support you by not giving you my honest opinion, even when I believe in my heart I'm right?"

"We are Prophets. The line between right and wrong is already blurred."

"And still there are rules!" Leaf said firmly. "Kelly will ruin you if you allow her to stay here. And even though I'm not feeling Isabel because of that crazy episode when she tried to stab me in the neck, she spent all last night begging for forgiveness. At least she shows me she's trying to change. But my aunt is here to destroy you."

Isabel was remanded to the institute after a violent episode where she crawled on Leaf while he slept in bed with Nine and held a knife to his throat. Something that was hard to forget.

"So because Isabel kissed your ass it's okay for her to stay now?"

"Let's be clear. They all kiss my ass," Leaf said firmly. "But it was Isabel's eyes that let me know that at least she's trying. But Kelly is still hateful and angry as ever, if not worse." He sat up and rolled toward her. Placing a hand over hers he said, "Don't let her stay in our home, Nine. For once I'm begging for something. You granted everyone's wishes but mine."

"She has cancer."

He removed his hand. "She's a fucking liar," he barked.

"Leaf, please." She turned away from him.

"So you willing to let this destroy us?"

Silence.

He stood up. “I’m going to check on my pups.”

“When you going to check on your son?”

“How you sound? I spend plenty time with Magnus, but you too busy to see that because you’re catering to your mother’s trifling ass. Do you know she the one pissing all over the place? Like a cat.” He slipped into his grey sweatpants and white t-shirt before walking out the door.

NINE

Nine sat in the den where she spent most of her time with Kerrick when he was alive, looking over at Isabel and Kelly. She was sipping a glass of Francesca wine.

“When I was forced to kill Alice, I told myself I could never trust another family member where history has shown me how they really are. And yet I find myself in another compromising situation.”

"Alice deserved everything she had coming," Isabel said.

Nine nodded before taking a deep breath. "I know, which is why I've decided to let you stay," Nine said softly. She had already spoken to her mother but after speaking with Leaf and telling him her plan, even though he didn't approve, her decision was final.

Isabel smiled widely, clapping her hands together once. "Thank you so much, cuz. You won't regret this, I promise. Having me on your team will save your life."

Nine giggled. "Okayyyyy."

Kelly on the other hand seemed reserved, almost as if the decision didn't matter either which way. "Thank you, daughter. And I promise to be better to you than I've ever been."

Isabel looked at her. "Is that right?"

Kelly smiled, finding her brand of crazy amusing. "My dear, niece, stay out of it."

Nine stood up and walked toward the window before turning back around and looking at them. "I've made many decisions in my life. Of great importance to many people. And this is the first time I'm concerned that it will have a negative impact on my marriage. So I need to know right now, from you both, am I making a mistake?"

Isabel stood up and gently held Nine's hand. "I can't say that I'm one hundred percent healthy, Nine. I don't know what that is like anyway because all of my life I've heard voices. But I can promise you that I'm doing better. And I hope this is enough."

Nine looked closely at Isabel and she could see what Leaf was saying. Her eyes were sincere but sad as if they were crying on the inside. Nine hugged her tightly. "I believe you, Izzy."

Releasing her, Nine looked over at Kelly who chose to remain seated. "I'm your mother, Nine. And a mother wants nothing but the best for her child. So I'm telling you with all my heart that I am here to be a blessing not a burden." She put her hand on her chest.

Nine walked over and sat next to her, touching her hand gently. On the surface it looked as if Kelly were being honest but it was hard to tell. She was too blinded by wanting Kelly in her life to see deeper. "Thank you, mother," Nine said hugging her. "Thank you."

As Nine submitted herself to Kelly's embrace it was Isabel who caught the glare on Kelly's face yet again.

And she didn't like it.

ANTONIUS

Antonius walked into the room, which held Alice's cell. Moving toward the bars he reached in with a paper bag, which included a fresh salad and tuna sandwich but today Alice was not receptive. Trying to connect wit her, Antonius opened the cell and placed the food on her bunk, exiting and closing it afterwards.

"So you ignoring me today?" He asked sitting across from the cell.

She turned away from him.

"Alice, please, look at me."

"Why? So you can continue to treat me like a zoo animal instead of a living breathing person?" She paused. "Speaking of animals, where's the dog you promised me?"

He sighed. “Turns out he hates me too much to give me one.”

“Whatever, it doesn’t matter.”

“I’m...I’m starting to have feelings for you.” He said out loud which had been the first time. “And I don’t know how to handle it.”

Alice turned around and walked toward the bars. She wiped the tears from her naturally blushed cheeks. “Then tell me how you feel. Let me hear those words instead of thinking that I’m going crazy for having feelings for you too.”

Antonius stood up and walked toward the bars, rubbing his fingers over hers as she gripped them tightly. Reaching into his pocket he removed the key and opened the door. Walking inside he stood in front of her, his height towering over her body like an oak tree, powerful but filled with love.

She looked down at herself, and slowly removed the buttons on the tattered baby blue blouse she wore, freeing her breasts. Next she slowly stepped out of the black sweatpants she was wearing totally exposed. Standing before him as vulnerable as she could be he observed her body. Her light skin flushed red due to the excitement of her blood rushing to the surface.

Carefully he came out of his white t-shirt first, followed by his jeans and boxers. His dick was stiff and pointed in her direction as if magnetized to her. Raising a hand she ran it over his warm brown chest. Slowly she lowered her head and kissed his muscular torso before looking up at him, begging him with her eyes to make love to her.

Not being able to take much more and being caressed by the soft scent of her musty pussy, he lifted her up and inserted himself into her body. Still on his feet, he controlled the efforts of his dick by pushing and pulling her softly onto him. Alice's already wetness spoke to the expert way he made love to her by releasing cream on his thickness.

Her body trembled and his stiffened as he experienced the power of a woman, something he surprisingly hadn't felt in a while. He didn't have a girlfriend. Lately Nine was a needy woman and all of his time, efforts and attention had gone to her, which he gladly did to be near her. But now, well now things were different.

He had grown tired of having to satisfy himself by grabbing a jar of oil and jerking off with the one thought he treasured above in his spank bank. The time he had accidently walked in on Nine lotioning her naked body in front of a mirror. Her fingertips ran slowly over each limb, leaving a silky coat on her chocolate skin. But when she bent down that day, causing her pussy to open like a rose, he always wondered if she knew he was there.

But now was all about Alice Prophet. Because after seeing her make love to Leaf he was finally realizing that he would never have Nine and that it was time to move on for good.

If only he wasn't doing it in such a deceitful way by being with Alice, he could rest easier. There was no way on earth Nine would ever approve of their relationship and he knew it. So their bond would always have to remain a secret.

Perhaps that's what made their moment, in the cell, so much more powerful. It was forbidden and they both were willing participants knowing all the while that if Nine ever saw them together it would be off with their heads.

Literally.

Slowly he walked her to the thin bunk and climbed on top of her warm body as he continued to power drive into her vanilla colored pussy. Her legs spread like scissors giving him complete access, neither knowing that once again Antonius had failed to lock the door.

And so, there Isabel stood, watching the entire seen as if it were an epic movie. At first thought her foolish mind was attempting to trick her again until it became obvious. Her cousin was alive and Antonius was in love.

ISABEL

Isabel stumbled up the steps and bumped into Kelly. Her mind was all over the place after witnessing her cousin making love to Antonius. Wondering what was wrong with her niece Kelly grabbed her by the shoulders roughly.

"Oh no, child." Kelly looked behind herself. "Your eyes say you've gone crazy again and I'm begging you to snap out of it before Nine finds out and sends us both back. For whatever reason your fate is tied up with mine at the moment and I have plans."

Isabel remained stiff, confused by it all. The fact that Alice was alive. The fact that Antonius was fucking the shit out of her and the fact that Nine had lied about killing her. Kelly could've been anyone for that moment because she was so stunned when she finally told her the secret.

"Isabel, what's wrong?" Kelly asked again, squeezing her harder.

"Alice...she's...she's alive!"

Stunned, Kelly released her. "What?"

ISABEL

Isabel stepped out of the shower after masturbating to the image of Antonius and Alice in her mind. She was debating on whether to confront Nine about Alice still being alive but she liked Antonius and realized that he would be thrown under the bus too, which is something she didn't want for him. Her goal was to only have the real ones around Nine and he was definitely it.

She was about to pick up her habit from the wet bathroom floor when Porter came up behind her and squeezed her tits.

"What is wrong with you, boy?" She yelled slapping his hands off of her. "Are you crazy or something?"

"I was trying to catch a feel," he laughed.

"How many times do I have to tell you I'm not interested?"

"You can tell me as many times as you want, niece. I'm still going to try my hand at that pussy."

"You know what, get your ass out of here, Porter! Now!"

"I will but I'll be back." He paused. "I'm gonna convince you that you belong to me sooner than later. Or wear you down trying." He walked out the door and she shook her head before smiling.

Just that quickly Alice was out of her mind.

CHAPTER SIX

LISA

"Forever and a day."

- William Shakespeare

Holding her stomach after Wagner and Jeremy punched her repeatedly, bruising her inner organs, Lisa stumbled toward Nine's bedroom door ready to tell it all. For years Lisa had endured the abuse of her brothers when for whatever reason they chose to act out their anger by hitting her and sometimes her son. In the beginning she didn't know where the anger originated but after time it became clear.

Although Kerrick senior was rarely around when he was alive, when he did visit it was Lisa who garnered all of his affections. She got the extra money if he brought some to spare. She received extra gifts just because she was beautiful. And most of all, she received the most of Kerrick's warped expressions of love. And although Wagner and Jeremy would never admit it, they hated her during those moments.

Now it was time to tell another soul. The great Nine Prophet. She knew her mother would never be strong enough to handle it because she also had a favorite. Jeremy. So Lisa telling her that he was part monster too wouldn't go over well.

But Nine, well she was different. She was a rescuer and Lisa felt comfortable telling her. When she built up enough energy she took a deep breath and grabbed the doorknob. But before entering she was yanked back and when she looked behind her she was staring up at Antonius.

He closed the door softly so that Nine, who was staring out the window when the door opened, wouldn't see or hear them. Then he grabbed Lisa's hand and whisked her off to his room within the house. With the door closed he got right down to it.

"Were you just downstairs again?" He whispered. He had forgotten to lock the door and when he finished making love to Alice he noticed it was partially open. He had no idea that it was Isabel who had seen it all.

"What?" She said holding her stomach. "What are you talking about? I wasn't downstairs."

He eyed her closely. "Then what were you doing going to Nine's room just now?"

"I...uh...wanted to talk to her." She paused. "About something private."

"I know that, but about what?"

Lisa looked around the room, which was not decorated and felt cold. Antonius had a daughter off the property and spent his free time there with her even though she hated him. As a result, he never made the room feel like home.

"Like I said it's private," she said rubbing her belly again.

Antonius sighed. "Listen, I know you don't understand what you saw some time back and I'm sorry but I can't allow you to tell Nine. I just can't."

"What does that mean?"

"It means I'm willing to do whatever I must to keep you quiet."

She understood the threat now. "I promise," she sat on the edge of the bed, a firm hand to her belly. "I wasn't about to talk to her about that."

He moved closer and this time considered her with a more scrutinizing eye. "What's wrong then? Are you hurt?"

"Like you would care."

He walked away and leaned against the wall. "Listen, I know you may think I'm the enemy but it's not the case. There are just some...I mean...it's hard to explain."

"So don't." She snapped and then took a deep breath. "I'm sorry. I just have a lot on my mind." She sighed. "I have a question. Even if it was a family member, do you think Nine would throw someone out if one person was hurting the other?"

He took one step closer and stuffed his hands into his pockets. "It depends."

"On what?"

"On how severe and to who."

She rubbed her stomach. "You mean for instance, if the harm was done to someone who has been around longer versus somebody like me?"

"No, I just mean Nine has a way of handling each situation. And I can't pretend to know all her ways because she's complex." He scratched his baldhead. "For the most part she doesn't like injustices of any kind. And I do believe she wants everything to work out for everybody here. But she has an inner code that she moves by. A code that if you push the wrong numbers could mean everything would blow up in your face. Whatever you want to tell her just be careful."

NINE

Dressed in a white tracksuit that hugged her curves, Nine walked into the backdoor of her house. She had just finished jogging and wanted to talk to Antonius about the drug operation, something she hadn't bothered to do in weeks. But when she entered door after the other she didn't see him and was growing agitated.

"What is it with the men in my life?" She said to herself. "Am I losing hold of them all?"

She thought about going to the basement but wanted to make that her last resort. Alice set her off in ways she didn't want to admit and on a deeper level she felt bad for keeping her flesh and blood hostage, while still being too angry to let her go.

She was about to look deeper into the house when she walked toward his room and saw him coming out with Lisa. Neither of them saw her as they whispered to one another. Confused, she wiped the sweat off her face and approached him when Lisa walked away.

"Where were you?" She asked.

"Oh...I was just taking a nap."

Her heart thumped. Her precious Antonius lied to her face and so effortlessly at that. "Are you rested?"

"Yeah." He smoothed his goatee with his hand and crossed his muscular arms over his chest. "Of course."

She moved closer. "Antonius, a lot is going on in my life right now. More than I care to admit. But understand this, I can't lose you too."

"And you won't." He dropped his arms at his sides. "Never."

"You are very correct but not for the reasons you think." She paused and wrapped her arms around his waist, nestling her face into his chest. "I will not lose you because I won't let you go. And if I'm forced to let you go for another, I will grow violent to you both." She looked up at him. "You do understand this right?"

He nodded.

She smiled, released him and walked away.

LEAF

Leaf opened the refrigerator and grabbed a tray of cold cut sandwiches the chef made earlier. Ready to grub hard, he sat it on the table in the kitchen and was preparing to dig in when Antonius walked up to him. "How you doing, man?" Antonius asked.

"Listen, you helped me with the birth of my pups but we not friends." Leaf grabbed one of the sandwiches and took a big bite. "Now leave me be. You spoiling my appetite."

Antonius took a deep breath. "So you going to hate me forever?"

"What you want from me, man?" Leaf asked harsher. "We not friends and we never gonna be. It ain't right that I should be anyway with the nigga who wants to fuck my wife."

"And that's what I want to talk about."

Leaf figuring Antonius was finally about to come clean dropped his sandwich on the counter brushed his hands and moved toward him. "And what exactly do you gotta say to me, nigga?" His nostrils flared. Antonius had a few inches on him easily but Leaf could care less.

"That I think something's wrong. With Nine."

Leaf laughed, shook his head and walked back toward the platter. "Yeah, well I already know that." He picked up his sandwich and took another bite.

"Listen, I don't know everything that happened when Nine was in this house, forced to live beneath it, but I do know the woman I met when she was free ain't the woman I'm seeing now."

"And you telling me this because?"

"Because it's time to start being there for her, man. Put your ego aside." Antonius took a deep breath and moved closer. "Listen, I don't agree with all the shit ya'll got going on. Brothers with sisters, cousins with cousins. It's no wonder ya'll don't have two heads."

"And we not asking you to understand."

"I get that. But all I'm saying is you need to do a better job seeing about your wife. Else we all in trouble." Antonius knocked on the counter once and walked away.

Leaf continued to chew his meal but suddenly his appetite was ruined. He tossed the sandwich across the kitchen and ran his hand down his face before sighing deeply.

He knew Antonius was right but bitterness had already started sitting in his organs, causing him to pump hate twenty four seven. But he also knew how violent Nine could get if she was left to her own accord for too long. He'd seen her cut niggas down for little and didn't want her going berserk. So he made a decision, to get right with his wife after he saw about his pups.

Walking downstairs, toward the room, he heard a noise inside that sounded like a whelp. Pushing the door opened he saw four of his pups surrounding the other along with their mother. When he moved closer it was obvious that one was dead, its neck turned in the opposite direction of its body.

Stumbling backwards, he fell down, placed his face into his palms and screamed. "NINEEEEEEEEE!"

CHAPTER SEVEN

NINE

"Black Macbeth will seem as pure as snow."

- William Shakespeare

Guilt was heavy in Nine's heart.

Easing out of bed, she walked toward the window where Porter and Leaf were digging a small hole in the yard for the puppy she'd murdered. In a moment of jealous rage, she didn't have control over her actions, being moved solely by her ego. Her ego, which at the moment was out of touch of the love and person she was trying to be. And even in the moment she still feared herself. Because yes it was wrong to kill such a precious animal but she would do more if things didn't start going her way.

That was certain.

"God, please help me stop," she whispered.

"What you talking about, child?" Kelly said walking up behind her.

Nine turned around, smiled and walked to the bar she had in her room. "Want something to drink?"

"In the morning?"

Nine shrugged. "Why not?"

"Nah, I can't with the pills I'm taking for my cancer."

"That brings me to another point. I'm going to have Bridget take you to the best doctors."

Kelly's eyes widened. "But I don't want—"

"I will not take no for an answer." Nine nodded and made herself a martini with olives before taking a seat on the daybed by the window. "Mother, are you peeing around the house?"

"What? Of course not! It's probably Leaf's dogs."

"Maybe." She paused. "Settling in okay, mother?"

"Yes, but I'm worried about you."

"Why?" Nine took a sip.

"Because I fear what I didn't want to happen is happening now."

Nine took another sip. "Meaning?"

"I know you loved Fran more than you ever did me. And I know she did things for you that I could never do at the time of my weakness. But there was one thing I knew about being in this family. One thing that unless you lived it you could never understand."

"And what's that?"

"That they are naturally drawn to a certain type."

"Mother, I'm confused."

"Look around you, Nine. Everyone and I do mean everyone, has skin the color of vanilla except you. And I hate to admit it but I fear you've fallen out of Leaf's favor because of it." She took a deep breath. "This was the reason I used to bleach your skin back in the day, so that you could stay desirable. Not because I didn't love you, but because I did."

Nine sat her martini glass down on the floor, eased up and walked toward the other side of the room. Her mother's words cutting into her skin like Kerrick's whip when he used to torture her. "That's not true. Leaf loves how I look."

"Then what other reason could it be that he is no longer interested? The Prophets talking, Nine. And I've seen Leaf look at Lisa with admiration. She is redbone which is, and will always be, a Prophet preference."

Nine shook her head several times. "No, no, that's not true."

Kelly stood up and walked toward her. Placing a hand on her shoulder she said, "Maybe I'm wrong. But ask yourself, what if I'm right? Do you really want women in your home who your husband would prefer over you?" She kissed her on the cheek and walked out the door.

LISA

Lisa walked carefully down the long corridor leading toward her room when Jeremy and Wagner approached. Wagner placed a long strand of hair behind her ear and smiled. "So I heard you been trying to talk to Nine." He grinned. "Tell me, sis, what's that about? Me playing with you a little?"

Lisa shook her head rapidly. "I'm just going to get my baby and—"

"Our baby," he corrected her. "I think you forget far too much so now I have to remind you."

"That's true, Lisa," Jeremy said. "You keep acting like he just yours and that be getting Wagner mad. Maybe that's why he has to put you in line. Right, twin?"

"Exactly." He sucked his teeth. "But she knows how that makes me feel. Don't you, baby girl?"

"I'm not telling anybody anything."

"I know you won't." Wagner stepped closer. "Because you know what's good for you and—"

"What's going on here?" Antonius asked approaching the siblings.

Wagner cleared his throat and stuffed his hands in his back pockets. Jeremy, always a follower, did the same. "Nothing, we were just talking to my girlfriend." Wagner said.

Antonius, immediately disgusted since they were brother and sister, tried to exit the thought from his mind. "Well how 'bout ya'll go on ahead about your business."

Wagner said, "But we were—"

"I said bounce!" Antonius roared.

Wagner and Jeremy disappeared down the hallway, leaving them alone. "How are you?" He asked thinking he saved the day.

"I wish you hadn't done that," she said, huge tears rolling down her cheeks.

"They're the ones hurting you aren't they? The ones you were going to tell Nine about?"

She moved closer, so that only he could hear her words. “Listen to me. My life was never cushy. I come from a very abusive background and you just made things worse for me and my son.” She took a deep breath and looked down. “Antonius, please don’t worry. I will keep your secret about whatever goes on downstairs. But I’m begging you to please stay the fuck away from me!” She stormed off.

LISA

Lisa was exhausted and scared when she walked into the nursery. It was her turn to help her mother with the Prophet children as she, Samantha, Bethany and even Noel rotated. She also wanted her child.

When she walked in to get her son she was devastated when she saw Wagner holding a picture in one hand and Kerrick II in the other. The toddler was trying his best to get away by wiggling and screaming but it didn’t work.

"What are you doing?' She asked. "Please don't hurt him."

"Be honest. Is he mine?" He asked looking at the photo of Kerrick and then the child's adorable face.

"Yes. Of course he's yours." She took one step closer.

"You don't have to lie. I don't fuck with the little nigga either which way. Might as well tell the truth."

"He's yours."

"Hey," Bridget said walking in the door with Jeremy. She was holding Magnus and Jeremy was holding the hands of Denarius and Julius.

Wagner walked up to Lisa and grabbed Lisa's hand. "Hey, mom," he said. "We were just playing with Kerrick. We about to leave though."

Kerrick II ran up to Denarius and Julius as they began to play with a red ball in the room.

"Where are you guys going?" She asked. "I thought it was your day to help me with the kids, Lisa."

"It is but..."

Wagner squeezed her hand tightly, silencing her. He cleared his throat and said, "I'm just gonna show her something right quick. We be back."

"Can I go?" Jeremy asked.

"Nigga, you gotta help ma." He paused. "Let's go, Lisa." He pulled her out the door.

With her fingers still clutched in his palm he led her to a room no one frequented but him. Since it was on the lower level, and facing the vineyard, it was hard to control the spiders and so they were everywhere. Until they could get them under control they elected to close the room out.

Cobwebs hung in the corners of the walls and it was virtually empty. Walking deeper into the room they moved to the grim yellow rusty bathroom. Once inside he closed the door and clutched his hands in front of him.

"So Antonius is your nigga right? He saving the day or whatever? You giving him my pussy too?"

Lisa remained silent choosing not to anger him anymore. Instead she pushed down her blue jeans and pulled her white t-shirt over her head. She followed it up with her bra and panties.

When she was done she crawled into the rusty tub filled a little with dirty water and waited. A minute later Wagner pushed his pants and boxers down before he crawled inside also. Standing over her, within seconds she felt warm urine trickling on her stomach neck and then face.

When he stopped she crawled on her knees. Face wet she looked up at him with hate.

"Bitch, I know you not crazy enough to try me."

"No. But one day when you least expect it someone will walk up behind you and put a bullet in the back of your—"

SLAP!

She held her throbbing face.

"Suck my dick, bitch. I ain't bring you hear to talk."

NINE

With her fourth martini in hand and a whip and handcuffs in the other, Nine strolled up to the door holding her cousin Alice inside. She hadn't been in the room in almost a year but for some reason she was in the mood.

When she opened the door the first thing that caught Nine off guard was the excited way that Alice approached the bars when she heard someone enter. A wide smile covered Alice's face and she oozed joy like a woman in love.

Nine's stomach fluttered instantly with anger.

Was Leaf coming down in the middle of the night to satisfy her cousin? Because he damn sure hadn't been checking for her. Who in the mansion had been giving Alice something to hope for when in Nine's mind she deserved nothing but pain?

The moment Alice recognized who was present she backed away from the cell and flopped on her bunk. "Hello, Nine." She trembled.

Nine placed the martini and whip on the chair and walked up to the cell with the cuffs. "Grab the bars, bitch."

"What's this about?"

"You gonna make me tell you again?"

Slowly Alice approached the bars, looking at the door as if she were expecting help. Within seconds Nine clicked the cuffs on her wrists, connecting her to the cell door. Afterwards, Nine dug into her pocket, removed the big key and opened it. Walking behind Alice she pushed down her pants, leaving her meaty ass cheeks bare.

"Fuck was you smiling about, whore?" Nine asked through clenched teeth. "You a prisoner. What you got to be happy about?"

"Nine, please, whatever you're about to do I'm begging you not to." Alice continued. "Please."

"You're begging me huh?"

"Yes." She cried.

"Well it sure as hell don't sound like begging to me." Nine paused. "Now let me hear you beg harder. The proper way."

"Nine, I—"

"BEG, BITCH!!!!!"

Alice's breath quickened. "Nine, I'm begging you please don't hurt me. And if I could be down on my knees right now I would. Now I know you hate me and—"

"You don't know shit about me, whore!" Nine continued. "Nothing!"

Nine walked out of the cell and reentered with the whip. Swinging wide, the first lick cut into Alice's fleshy yellow cheeks, causing blood to pour from the wound and down the back of her thighs. Having flashbacks on how Kerrick used to beat her, she struck her again and again until blood splattered on the floor, Alice's cries in the air.

Nine struck her repeatedly until she was so exhausted she could barely stand up. What startled Nine in that moment were two things. First, that she was more relieved than she had been before she entered and secondly how wet she was afterwards. Maybe she was as sick as Kerrick after all.

Tired, and feeling better already, she strutted around and looked at Alice. "Are you fucking, bitch?"

Alice shook her head many times. "No, cousin. I'm not. I promise."

"I don't believe you."

"But I promise you I'm not having sex." Alice breathed heavily.

"Let me be clearer. What's mine is mine, and if I find out that you are coming in the way of that I will pull out my black book filled with torture ideas you can't even imagine." She whispered in her ear. "Understand, cousin?"

"Yes. I do."

CHAPTER EIGHT

ISABEL

"Therefore, since brevity is the soul of wit."

- William Shakespeare

Isabel stood on her knees, hands pressed together in prayer on the side of her bed in Fran's room. The violent thoughts that accompanied her mind never left and yet she managed to ignore them at least up until that moment.

Still, the demons wanted Kelly Prophet dead and she was kind of feeling the idea.

"Father, please keep me sane. I don't want to be what people think I am. I want to be what You want me to be. But I need some help. Please."

"Izzy," Nine said entering Fran's room. "What are you doing in here? And why are you wearing the habit?"

Isabel stood up, sat on the edge of the bed and smiled holding her hand. "It makes me feel comfortable and safe to be here and in this."

Nine didn't want anyone in Fran's room, let alone her clothing, but at least there was another person on earth who found peace in Fran's space even though Isabel barely knew Fran. "Is everything okay, Izzy?"

Not wanting to be trouble Isabel nodded. "Yes, cousin. Things are fine."

From where she was Nine scanned the small room. "Have you seen Leaf?"

"No cousin, I haven't. Have you?"

"No."

Nine sat next to Isabel and gripped her hand, both looking ahead at the open door. Finally Isabel turned toward her and considered every feature of Nine's beautiful face. "Why do you think God made you so pretty?" Nine, thinking she was mocking, snatched her hand away. "Did I say something wrong?"

"You don't have to do that." Nine walked across the small room. "I don't require compliments. I already said you could stay."

"What do you mean?" Isabel asked, standing up to approach. "I'm speaking truth."

"But it's not true."

Isabel looked at her for a moment and then busted out into insane laughter. "Wow, here I am concerned that the crazy demons were after me and you are even worse off than I am."

"Isabel, stop it with all this stupidness!"

"But I can't." Suddenly Isabel grew serious as she stepped in front of her. "Tell me one time, just one, where you've known me to say things I don't mean. I'll wait."

Nine searched her mind and couldn't find one moment. In fact Isabel's ability to say just what she was thinking at all times made her somewhat socially awkward. "But mother thinks I'm too dark and—"

Isabel glared. "Let me tell you something right now. Everything about you is perfection." She grabbed her hand and looked down at how their fingers intertwined. The dark chocolate and vanilla smoothed together on top of one another like a sundae. "What's prettier than your tone, especially when it's next to mine?"

Nine walked away and flopped on the bed. "But...Leaf isn't...he isn't responding to me anymore."

"That doesn't mean he doesn't want you."

"But mother thinks it is."

Isabel took a deep breath. She was tiring of that whore and the feeling was mutual with Kelly. "Do you remember what father used to do to me?"

Nine nodded yes, because everyone knew. People considered Isabel to be a sexual deviant but it was her father who started it all. Yes every nasty, vile and depraved feat imaginable she'd done. But it was only after being forced to do things against her will. Having her body used for pleasure by her father and his friends at age six and beyond, caused her to run cold emotionally.

"I remember what he did to you, although they gave me little details." Nine admitted. "I guess out of Prophet shame."

"The details aren't necessary. Just know that they were some of the darkest days of my life." Isabel sighed. "But what I also learned from my darker days was that my body may have been flesh but using my mind I could escape to anywhere. But sometimes," she touched Nine's hand again, "escape isn't good enough. Sometimes, you gotta get rid of the people who keep you in your darkest places first. Granddad did that when he killed Richard and you have to do that with your mother. She is evil. As pure as the color black."

"I don't understand."

"Yes you do." Isabel continued. "You're just not willing to do what it takes to let her go. But you will eventually because she'll leave you no choice. Strike first, Nine. Now!"

KELLY

Kelly sat in the sitting room of the mansion in front of Lisa, Jeremy, Wagner, Porter and Bridget in the same chair that Nine had when she laid down the law to her and Isabel. They were drinking green tea as she told them stories of the past, from when Kerrick was alive and living in Africa.

Sitting her gold-rimmed teacup on the saucer next to her, she took a deep breath and looked at them. "Father would definitely approve of you being here."

"What does that mean?" Bridget asked, taking another sip.

"For starters look at you all," she said brightly. "You're so light you could pass for white. The perfect combination for his plan and goals for the future." Porter laughed causing Kelly to frown. "What's funny?"

"Niggas ain't getting extra credit for being light skin these days. At the end of the day you go through the same problems as everybody else, no matter the tone. The only thing that can change things a little is money. Which we got." He looked at his mother and then his siblings. "Which is also why I don't understand why you fucking with the program."

Kelly nodded. "Okay, I understand you're—"

"You don't understand shit about me," Porter continued. "Now you may have my mother, brothers and sister's ears but you don't have mine. Plus Isabel warned me about your ass." He pointed at her.

"Isabel," Kelly repeated through clenched teeth. She was definitely getting on her nerves. "She doesn't know what she's talking about."

"Whatever. I know this, even listening to this conversation means treason." Porter stood up. "Don't worry, I won't tell Nine, but I'ma tell you now you wrong as fuck. Stay away from me." He stormed out.

"Porter!" Bridget screamed.

"Let him go," Kelly said calmly. "It's too much for him to hear that he deserves this money as much as Nine if not more. We are father's children not his grandchildren."

"If Daddy felt that way, why did he give her all the money?" Lisa asked. "If that was really something he was shooting for I don't understand."

Kelly sighed. "Because she seduced him in the night hours." She said growing agitated. "Like dark bitches do." She continued. "But don't worry, I have a plan that will put me where I need to be. In charge of it all. And I just need to know if you're in or you're out because when I rule there won't be another chance for you to jump on board. It's now or never."

CHAPTER NINE

NINE

"Thus conscience does make cowards of us."

- William Shakespeare

Nine sat in her room drinking brown liquor; something that was normally not her speed. But it was Leaf's drink so she decided to give it a try to be next to him anyway she could. When the door opened and Leaf walked inside, he looked at her and shook his head.

"Where have you been?" She asked as he moved to the corner of the room to remove his clothing. "I've been looking for you for over a day. Are you purposefully hiding from me in this house?"

Silence.

Nine sat the glass down on the end table. "So you aren't speaking to me now?"

"What you want me to say?" He responded, tossing his white t-shirt and grey sweatpants in the bin. The slit in his red boxers now providing a peek of his manhood. "That I know you killed one of my dogs and I'll never forgive you for it?"

"If it be true than yes." She paused. "Say it. Say something!"

He shook his head and laughed. "What kind of evil did it take, for you to pick up an innocent animal and break it's neck?"

She picked up the glass and drank what remained inside. "The kind that is growing weary from not getting attention from her husband. And the kind that can do much more if that doesn't change and soon."

He glared, his lips pressing closely together. "I didn't think it could be done but now I know that it can."

"And what does that mean?"

"I'm starting to fall out of love with you."

The glass fell out of her hand and crashed to the floor. In the moment, upon hearing his words, she was doing all she could to stay conscious. Her mother had warned her that she was no longer attractive to him and now she was realizing she was correct.

"You don't, you don't mean that," she whispered.

He walked toward the bathroom but stopped short of entering. Taking a deep breath he said, "When I look at you now all I can feel is the fact that you disgust me. And that's enough to make my dick soft." He entered the bathroom slamming the door.

With two fists drawn tightly she ran toward it, banging on the wood with all her might. "So what is it huh?" She yelled, spit flying from her lips as she remained in a drunken rage. "Is my skin not light enough for you? Am I not pretty enough for you? Do you prefer my cousin or Lisa? Huh? What is it?"

"Get the fuck from in front the door, bitch." Leaf continued before turning on the shower, drowning out her sound.

"I won't let you fuck Lisa! Do you hear me? I won't let you have her!"

"Nine," Lisa said entering the room, having heard it all. "Are you, are you okay?"

Nine, who was normally regal took a deep breath and raised her head high as if all were well. And still she looked like a mad woman. Her face wet with sweat and her eyes wild and crazy. "What...do...you...want?"

Lisa took a step inside and fiddled with her fingertips. "There's, I, I want to talk to you about your mother." She paused. "And what she's trying to do behind your back."

Nine stumbled to the bed, half drunk and barely lucid. “What could you possibly think you…you…could tell me about my mother, bitch? You don’t even know my mother. You know nothing.”

“I understand but she’s having a meeting about—”

“Have you always been told that you’re beautiful?” Nine asked as she considered her vanilla colored skin, her long flowing hair and her natural rosy cheeks with extreme jealousy. “Do men respond to you despite not caring about what you have to say?”

“Nine, I—”

She grabbed the bottle. “Remove yourself from my sight.” She poured herself another glass of Hennessy. “You disgust me.” She drank it all.

Devastated, Lisa ran out crying into the hallway. Despite the pain ripping through her aunt’s heart at the moment, Nine continued to drink until she got so fired up it was time to do what she had grown to love again.

Torture Alice.

ANTONIUS

Antonius sat on the edge of Alice's bed and placed ointment on the bruises Nine had inflicted on her some days back that were starting to heal. The rage he felt in that moment as he looked at what Nine had done surprised him.

Ever since he'd come into contact with Nine he loudly pledged his loyalty while silently pledging his love. And to know that Alice, a woman he was coming to feel deeply for suffered under her tyranny, enraged him.

"I wish you'd say something," Alice said as she winced when he touched the ripped skin from the flesh of her rear. "Your silence feels as harsh as these wounds. It's almost as if I'd done something wrong to you."

"Don't say that!" He said defiantly, before tossing the blood soaked cotton on the floor and standing up. "My words could never...ever do what she's done to you."

Alice sat up, carefully pulled up her pants and walked over to him. "I'm sorry. And you're right."

He moved away again, the guilt he was placing on himself felt as if someone had dropped a thousand pound brick on his heart. Why didn't he rescue the woman he claimed to love? Why was she still behind bars when he had the power to snatch her out, before running into the night? "What kind of man am I?"

"One that cares and—"

"No! I won't allow you to let me off this easily. I claim to care for you. To love you and then I allow her to keep you here and treat you like an animal."

Alice grabbed his hands and looked up at him. "No. Don't do this to yourself, Antonius. My being in here is a direct result of my actions and my actions alone. The only thing that keeps me sane is knowing this fact. Along with your love." She walked away and sat on the bed, wincing a little at the pain. "I did some awful things to her. Some really awful things."

"Like what?" He asked quietly, having heard vague stories from Nine but nothing concrete. "What could you possibly have done to make you feel like you deserve this? Tell me the worst incident, so that I can have some relief too. Because right now I feel like hurting her." He clenched his fists tightly and looked down at the weapons. “Something I would’ve never thought possible.”

She took a deep breath. “I’ve never said these things out loud. I think part of me took pleasure in playing the victim. I wanted the story to be that the evil Nine Prophet was holding me hostage for crimes I never committed. But that isn’t the case and it’s hard to know who’s right or wrong anymore.” She looked at him as he sat next to her. “But maybe if I tell you one story I remember I can finally be free.”

He nodded.

She looked outward, into the cell and recalled all of the things she’d done that she could remember.

“I was grandfather’s favorite. He spoiled me and gave me all of the trappings a queen would have.” She smiled remembering his love and gifts. “I was the standard by which grandfather compared every child born to his children. And somewhere I think I let it go to my head.” A tear rolled down her cheek.

“So knowing this, I inflicted my superiority on Nine. The darkest of us all.” She paused. “In the beginning I didn’t know she was under this house. But when I did find out she became my personal toy." She looked at him, her hazel eyes peering into his soul. "But there was one day that I tormented her that I knew I was building the monster she is today. And it scared me."

ALICE

THAT EVIL DAY

Alice was a sick young lady who like most Prophet women, had been molested by her father all of her life. So one day, with her mind out of control, she strutted into Nine's room holding a brown paper bag, closing the door behind herself.

"Hello, Number Nine." She taunted, as Nine was the ninth grandchild born of Kerrick's lineage. "How are you?"

Nine, petrified beyond belief trembled because Alice would not hold back on the brutality inflicted on her. For Alice it was all about physical, psychological and sexual torture combined.

"I brought food," Alice said, raising the bag. Since Nine barely ate the smell alone caused her body to tremble. "Hungry?"

Nine urinated where she stood, causing it to splatter to the floor. She wanted that food more than anything but she knew with it came the worst mental abuse imaginable.

"Oh my goodness, you've wet yourself again," Alice said realizing that the more afraid Nine was of her, the creamier her pussy grew. "Aren't you happy I came to visit you? Outside of that dirty maid," she said referring to Fran, "I know you don't have any friends. But thank God you can always count on me."

After waving the food in the air, knowing Nine would be hungry due to malnutrition, she removed a piece of fried chicken and said, "Lick it." And when Nine was about to bite it Alice warned, "If you bite it, bitch, I will kill you."

After allowing her to lick the salty crust without satisfying her hunger she said, "Now come lick my foot. And I'll give you a bite of my drumstick" Nine, preparing to walk over was quickly given the next set of rules. "Always approach me on your knees."

So Nine crawled and ran her tongue up and down the heel of Alice's foot before licking her toes in the hopes of getting the food. When she was done, Alice's foot was clean. And Alice, so turned on, raised her dress and played with her pussy until she exploded on her fingertips. Satisfied, she kicked Nine in the face and said, "Keep your fucking hands off of me! Before I tell grandfather on you! You know how much he loves me."

She left the room, leaving Nine humiliated, hurt and hungry.

ANTONIUS

PRESENT DAY

"That's just one instance but those types of things happened often," Alice said looking over at him to see how much he hated her.

Antonius, upon hearing the story felt confused. No he couldn't understand what would make a woman so demented and yet appear so forthcoming and changed. "Who are you now as a person, Alice?"

"I don't know." She replied.

Instead of being put off by her statement he considered her honesty refreshing. “It sounds like Kerrick tormented his entire family. People who are hurt, her others. And I know it doesn’t mean anything coming from me but I forgive you.”

Her eyes widened. “So you don’t think I’m a monster?”

“How could I?” He said placing his hand over hers. “We are victims of our environment. I mean, the world tries to pretend it’s not the case but it’s true. Society makes the monsters and then we pretend we had no part of the creation when shit gets violent.” He paused. “But I must know this, how do you feel about Nine now?”

Alice looked down. “I love her.”

Antonius looked into the center of her hazel eyes finding it hard to believe. “Despite all of this?”

“Yes.” She paused. “Because I understand why now. And if I’m ever free I would move on with my life and forgive her as you have forgiven me. And as I would one day want her to forgive me too.”

Deeper in love, Antonius leaned in and kissed her softly. His warm tongue rolling around the center of her mouth while her breasts pressed against his chest. He had fallen for a woman who could be deemed unlovable by some and evil by others and still he didn't care.

As they embraced in the cell, on the thin bunk, Nine opened the door and stumbled back when she saw the scene. Covering her mouth she tried to prevent from screaming. Her precious Antonius had betrayed her in the worse way possible.

He was sleeping with her enemy.

The anger, so powerful, coursed through every part of her body, even her clitoris. Reaching under the gown she wore she continued to watch in secret as she thumbed her clit softly, her juices pouring out over her red manicured nails. Antonius, oblivious to the silent audience, mounted Alice on top of him while Nine's anger only increased her sexual desire. Watching him pound into Alice with passion, Nine bit down on her lip causing a little blood to spill into her mouth.

Yes she satisfied herself from Antonius' deceit but it didn't mean that they both wouldn't pay.

NINE

Nine walked into Kelly's room and sat on the vanity chair with her as she watched her mother comb her long hair. Now Kelly definitely looked like money, dipped in diamonds and the like. "Mother, I'm, I'm deeply hurt. Beyond words even."

Kelly smiled.

Nine frowned. "So my pain brings you pleasure?"

"Of course not, daughter. But out of every great misery comes change. Even slavery didn't end until the north saw the south benefiting too much economically from free labor, causing Lincoln to step up and ignite the civil war." Kelly said proudly. "And I can tell by the look in your eyes that violent change is coming to Aristocrat Hills too."

Nine looked down, the cream of her recent indiscretions still on her fingernails. "I'm losing Leaf. And Antonius. I can't take a loss of both."

"I didn't know your heart spoke for Antonius."

"I didn't realize how much until now."

She nodded. "Well every man is always greater when he is sponsored by two loves. I don't see why this should be different for a woman." She paused. "So where is your attention now?"

"On Leaf. How do I get him back?"

Kelly put down her brush and turned toward her. "First you must empty your home for a few days." She touched Nine's face softly. "Give me some money and I will buy us all a block of rooms at the Four Seasons. So that you and your husband may have privacy."

"Then what?"

"Tomorrow, when you are all alone, make love to him with all the anger, love and passion you feel. And when he has weakened to you, and when he is under your spell, remind him of who you are."

"And who am I?"

"The Queen of the Prophet Empire."

"But what if he doesn't come home?"

"Then you'll know he isn't worthy." She paused. "Nine, you are a woman with the power to bring life and death to all under her reign. Remind him of these things and let him know that if he doesn't fall in line he will fall to death instead." Nine looked down and Kelly raised her head by way of her chin. "If you don't do this he will continue to misuse and take advantage of your kindness. It is the only way."

ISABEL

When Isabel saw Nine leaving Kelly's room she walked inside and slammed the door. Standing at the entrance she stared at Kelly as she continued to brush her hair. "What you doing, bitch?"

"Girl."

"You are trouble."

"Bye, child." Kelly giggled.

"What are you doing to Nine?"

Kelly laughed. "Don't tell me you have placed your lesbian crush on yet another cousin." She paused and looked over at her. "Alice is still alive. You saw with your own eyes. Go lick her pussy instead. I'm sure it hasn't been clean properly in years and could use the laps."

"What are you doing to Nine?" Isabel said firmer.

"Nothing. I told her what she needs to do to fight for her marriage. I'm not the bad guy, Isabel."

Isabel crossed her arms over her chest. "And how did you plan to help her get him back? You said you overheard Leaf telling Porter that he's leaving for a week tonight."

"I know." She shrugged. "So she'll do it when he comes back. After he's had time to cool off."

"Do you even love her?"

"You think because you're walking around in that habit it makes you holier than thou?" Kelly laughed. "Don't kid yourself, niecey pooh. You're still cuckoo and the world knows it."

"The difference between me and you is that I know I'm crazy. You still are under the illusion that you live in reality." She paused. "Pissing around the house and shit."

"I keep saying that isn't me!"

"I won't let you ruin her," Isabel said seriously. "While you play in the background I'll be working the front. She's the only person that's consistent in my life and I need her strong."

"Right now you're going to need to gather your things. Because while Leaf is gone to get his mind together Nine has instructed me to clear the house so she can do the same."

ISABEL

Isabel walked toward Nine's closed bedroom door and knocked lightly. She didn't believe a word her aunt said. Nine opened it and smiled although she looked emotionally drained. "Hello, Izzy."

Isabel grinned back, shocked by her pleasant demeanor. "Look, I just wanted to make sure you want us to leave tomorrow because you needed time for yourself."

"It's true."

Isabel stood corrected. At first she seriously thought Kelly was running game. "Oh because—"

"Izzy, I care for you. I really do. But now is not the time for a lot of questions. I'm fighting for my life and I need you to go with my mother tomorrow. She's taking care of everything."

"But I don't trust—"

"Izzy, is that clear?" Nine said louder. "I need you on my side with this so I can do what I can with Leaf tomorrow."

"But Leaf is going to—"

"Izzy, go away!" She yelled. "Now!"

Isabel looked down. "Okay, cousin. Whatever you say." She turned around and walked away.

NINE

Nine sat in her office, behind her desk when Antonius strutted inside. His cologne caught her senses and made her smile. *Damn this man is handsome.* "Hello, Antonius."

He nodded. "Hello." He cleared his throat and seemed colder to her than he had in the past. "What do you need, Nine?"

"I need you to leave."

His eyes widened. Now he wasn't so reserved. "Why?" He stepped further inside. "What did I do?"

"Nothing." She took a deep breath. "I'm taking a little me time and I want my house clear." She shrugged. "Nothing more or less."

He looked around, his mouth drying from worry. There was no way he wanted to see Alice alone without his watchful eye to protect her. He had even sent his daughter Sheena away to live with his aunt so that he could be at the mansion everyday for a few weeks. "But this place is huge."

"And still I want it empty."

"Nine, what about, what about Alice?"

Silence.

Nine didn't speak because she wanted him to stew in the sound of his own betrayal. Although he wasn't aware that she knew he had fallen for her cousin, she wanted him to be as uncomfortable as possible. "I don't understand the question, Antonius."

He scratched his baldhead and his throat bubbled as he paced. "I...I know you have a lot going on and, well, I just wanna know who's gonna feed her that's all."

"I am."

"But I don't want you to worry about her." He walked up to the desk. "While you're getting yourself together I don't mind looking after her and the mansion. I'll stay out of your hair I swear. You'll never hear or see me."

Yeah because you'll be knee deep in the pussy. She thought.

Now she was livid. Nine's anger boiled to a dangerous level. "Is something going on with you and my cousin?" She stood up and walked around her desk. "Something I should know about?"

"What?" His eyes widened. "Of course not. I—"

"Then don't question me. *Ever.* Now leave, Antonius." He nodded, turned around and walked toward the door. "Listen, I know you're spending a lot of time with her," she continued. "But she isn't who she claims to be. If she's ever free the first person she would try to kill is me."

He turned around. "And I would never let that happen."

"Are you sure?"

He took a deep breath. "I'm positive." He walked back over to her. "And you're right. I have had small conversations with Alice. And because of it I can sense her goodness."

"Her goodness?" She giggled. "The woman is the anti-christ."

"Yes, but if ever there was a time I thought you were in danger than I would take her head off with my bare hands." He paused. "I mean that with all my heart."

Nine walked up to him, gently grabbed his hand and placed it over her chest. She looked up at him. "Do I still have your undying loyalty?"

"Of course."

She let him go. "I hope so. Because soon there will come a time where you'll have to prove it. Of this I am sure." Nine walked around her desk and sat in her seat. "Now go. You're dismissed."

Head low, he trudged out.

CHAPTER TEN

NINE

"The cat will mew and the dog will have his day."

- William Shakespeare

The mansion was empty.

Everyone left in black Mercedes Sprinters earlier in the day headed away to where Kelly had rented suites at the Four Seasons in Baltimore. And now, with the help of her staff and a chef, Nine planned a romantic evening for her cousin. She told herself that this would be the night where their marriage would change for the better and in fact she prayed on it.

Besides, she was tiring of arguing with him about what had become of their lives and she was willing to make some sacrifices as long as he understood that she was in a bind. Their family needed her and she needed them. The last thing she wanted was to see people out on the street, not when she had the space and means.

When the meal was prepared Nine showered and smoothed cocoa butter all over her skin. She glistened under the soft yellow lights of her mansion as she walked to the dining room, excited about what the evening would hold for them. Their bed sheets had been changed and scented with hints of lavender and soft candles glowed throughout.

In the dining room a red tablecloth dressed the table which signaled love and Nine ordered that the wooden slats on the table be removed so that it was smaller and she could sit closer to Leaf.

With everything in order she decided it was time to walk to the portion of the mansion Leaf stayed, a room off the west corridor. When she arrived to the door she knocked softly.

No answer.

Again she knocked lightly before going harder. Again no answer. She wasn't surprised in the least. Leaf would often sit on the other side of the door, refusing to answer for her or anybody else for that matter.

"Leaf, I know you are in there. And I know you're listening." She paused. "I can't imagine what you're going through, not being able to have our relationship be private like you always wanted. But tonight I'm willing to talk about how I can make you happy. Please, *please* come out and spend time with me," she begged. "I've sent everyone away."

Silence.

"Leaf, please open up to me. I can't save our marriage alone."

Silence.

"Leaf?" She twisted the knob and entered. When she glided inside it was unreasonably cold. Walking to the open window she closed it and as she glanced around something became evident; he hadn't been there all day. When she looked at the closet the few outfits he brought from their room were gone and in the place were empty hangers.

Something was wrong!

Leaving his room she walked to the dogs den in the basement and was devastated when she saw the animals were also missing. That's when she felt a brick in her stomach. Had Leaf left the home for a moment or a lifetime?

"Leaf," she said to herself. "Please, not like this." Immediately she was pushed back to the first day they met.

THE DAY THEY MET

Nine, who was a dirty Prophet secret, was with Fran when Leaf wandered down to the basement while his father Justin met on a rare visit with his father Kerrick upstairs. Fran who had left the door unlocked by accident was shocked to see the handsome young man with yellow skin and curly hair staring at them. He had never been there before.

Although Fran tried to get rid of him he wouldn't go, his eyes glued on the woman's whose skin glowed so beautifully it looked like melting chocolate. After some efforts, eventually she was forced to leave them alone.

"Is your name really Nine?" Leaf asked when they were by themselves. He overheard someone calling her that name.

Nine, dirty and in tattered clothing, was stunned silent because she was always warned about the dangers of speaking to outsiders.

"So you really don't talk?" Leaf continued, finding her beyond beautiful.

Although she wore a saggy nightgown, her body was formed and Leaf noticed it all. Nine's hair was soft, wild and curly which added to her unique appeal. And Leaf desperately wanted to get to know the scraggly looking girl but he wasn't certain with her chocolate complexion if she was a part of the family. He wasn't interested in their incestuous ways.

"Since you won't talk, I'll call you Silent Nine."

Again she remained quiet. Realizing he wasn't getting anywhere with her his eyes scanned the room and suddenly his nose caught up with the faint odor of urine. There wasn't a window and without the glowing lamp it would be pitch black.

Was she being held hostage?

"Do you live down here?" He asked.

Silence.

"Why won't you talk to me?" He continued.

Nine walked away and sat on her bed as she awaited his next question. Her belly fluttered whenever she looked at him and when he caught her glances she'd turn away. His presence freshened the room and aroused the warm space between her legs that she was becoming familiar with each passing day.

"I get it," he grinned. "You want me gone. So just answer me this one question and I'll leave."

He held her attention.

"Are you a Prophet?" He asked.

She shook her head no because in a sense she was correct. Her mother, Kelly, told her repeatedly that she was Number Nine. Nothing more. Nothing less.

He smiled as if relieved. Now it would be easier to fall for a woman who was not his relative. "Okay."

When he was preparing to leave she parted her lips slowly. Licking the dryness away she said, "Please don't tell anyone you've been here."

He spun around until he was looking at her beautiful face again. Her voice sounded like blue water. "What did you just say?"

"I said please don't tell anyone that you were here or that you talked to me," she repeated. "It will be bad. For me."

He smiled. "I'll keep the secret on one condition."

"Anything," she said softly.

"That you talk to me when I come back."

"I don't know if I should do that," she admitted. "I just want to be left alone."

"For some reason, I can't promise you that," Leaf replied. "Being in this house every day is fucking with my head and you're the most interesting thing I've seen in a long time." Leaf walked toward the door and turned the doorknob. "I won't tell anyone I was here or that I talked to you, but I will be back whether you speak to me or not." With that he walked away knowing he had just met the new love of his life.

Nine, overcome by his presence dropped to her knees and exhaled. The entire time he'd been there, he had taken her breath away.

PRESENT DAY

After remembering their lives together Nine realized things would not be the same if he were gone. Having to deal with losing the man who saved her made for a dismal existence. After all, it was because of him she lived. And now that he had gone she had been burned to the core.

Now it was time to let loose her rage.

ALICE

Alice sat in the corner of the cell with the cell phone that Antonius snuck to her pressed against her ear. “No, she hasn’t come down all day.” She whispered making sure to look at the door every so often. “But I’m so afraid without you, Antonius. Something feels wrong.”

“I know.” He sighed. “But I’m going to do my best to get through to Nine. To let her know that you should be free. And that you’ve changed.”

“But what if she doesn’t listen? What if she doesn’t care?”

He took a deep breath. “Then I will pull you out myself.”

Alice held her stomach. Part of her wanted to call the police but that would unearth everybody’s funky secrets, including her own. “You would, do that for me?”

“I would do that for us.”

"Antonius, I don't think I can let you. I mean Nine is dangerous. You of all people should know what she could do if she feels betrayed. It's the reason I'm in this cell to begin with. And if something happened to you I don't, I don't think I would be able to breathe. I would kill myself."

"Don't say that!"

"It's true. I don't want anything happening to you because of me."

"Listen, Alice, I'm a man. And a strong one at that." He paused. "Now I want you to hear me out. Even if for some reason something happened it would never be your fault. Do you understand this?"

"I just..."

"Listen, Alice. I love you. I will be fine."

"Oh no," Alice whispered when she heard a sound beyond the closed door. "I think she's coming now."

"Call me back when—"

Alice ended the call abruptly and stuffed the phone under her pillow. Walking to the bars she looked at Nine who was dressed beautifully, believing that night that she would be with her husband, not Alice.

"Cousin," Alice said softly. "Will today be better?" She asked, pleading with her eyes for mercy.

Nine pulled a chair closely to the bars and sat down. "Sit."

Alice grabbed the only chair in her cell and pulled it closely to the bars. "Yes, cousin." She took a seat.

"Are you in love?"

Alice unconsciously placed her hand on her chest to slow down her breath and immediately Nine had all the answers she needed. "No...how could I be when I've been in here for two years?"

"Oh there are many ways. Aren't there?"

Alice looked away. "No, I mean yes but...I'm not doing anything. I'm just a prisoner meant for your pleasure."

Nine smiled. "Remove your pajama pants."

Slowly Alice removed her clothing.

"Spread your legs."

Alice complied.

"Wider."

Alice opened her legs as far as they could go. Now, from where Nine sat she got the perfect view. A clear sight of the pussy that had her best man betray her. "Now, put your index finger on your clit."

Relieved not to be beaten, she quickly obliged.

"Now flip your clit while I tell you a story."

Alice's eyes widened. "Cousin, I don't understand."

"Just do it!"

"Okay, okay." Alice nodded rapidly.

"This is the tale of a Bitch, A Ruler and A Servant." Nine paused. "Once upon a time a bitch lived under the stairs," Nine said, as she watched Alice rub herself. "And that Bitch was beaten almost everyday in the beginning and less as time went on." Alice continued to stroke. "Well one day the Bitch's Ruler had grown tired of her. And so the Ruler put her most humble Servant in charge of the Bitch." Alice rubbed a little harder and Nine noticed. "Well one day the Servant confessed his love for the Bitch and came to her cell, licked her pussy softly at first and then harder until the Bitch juiced up with pleasure. Afterwards, of course, they fucked."

As Nine watched Alice's pussy she saw a soft glisten come through, courtesy of the pleasure Alice was receiving when she thought of Antonius. Nine knew the last thing Alice wanted was to be turned on by the story but she was so deviant that Nine knew it was in her nature. And she was right.

"And when the Ruler found out, about the Servant's disloyalty, she went to the Servant's home with five soldiers and submitted one request." Nine paused. "OFF WITH HIS HEAD!"

Alice's hand dropped and long tears rolled down her cheek. She knew one thing above all in that moment. That Nine was onto her and Antonius.

"Alice, don't mistake my inaction when it comes to you as weakness. This house and this family forced softness out of me a long time ago." She paused. "If you continue...if you offer your body to him just once more... he will be but an after thought and so will you. Am I clear?"

When Nine was finished, taking the phone with her, she left. Alice was so devastated she considered one thought, that upon hearing the horrible news, lashes would have been better.

CHAPTER ELEVEN

NINE

"That is not passion's slave, and I will wear him in my heart's core, ay, in my heart of heart."

- William Shakespeare

Nine sat outside on her deck overlooking the vineyard when Kelly strolled outside holding a glass of Francesca wine. "This is okay," Kelly said, as she thought of the woman who had stolen her daughter's heart. "A little too tart for my taste." She placed the glass down and walked over to where Nine stood, taking a deep breath. "But it will do for some."

"What about your cancer? Bridget said you didn't want to go to the doctors."

"I'll go alone. And one glass of wine won't hurt."

Silence.

"So what is the verdict?" Kelly asked. "How was your evening with Leaf?"

"Leaf has left our home." She paused. "Didn't even say goodbye."

Kelly smiled out of view of Nine. "And how do you feel?"

"Lost."

Kelly nodded and leaned on the railing next to Nine, overlooking their vast land. "Feeling lost is a useless emotion. If you are going to move on, and move on you must, you must first get control over your home."

Nine glanced at her with confusion. The only thing that truly bothered her now was not having her man and because of it she was like a wounded animal with no place to hide. "I don't know what you mean."

"You are fragile now, Nine. And that means people will try you while you're in this state. Do you want them to take your estate too?"

Nine shook her head no. Being led solely by her mother, she had relinquished the power of her mind. Taking a deep breath she said, "Leaf is gone. I won't have them take my home too."

Kelly smiled. "Good, then that means it's time for order."

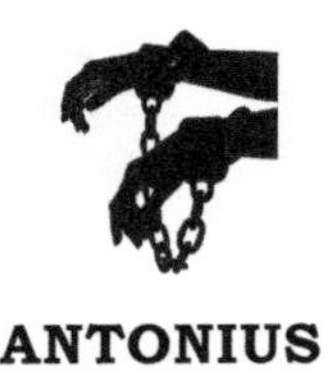

ANTONIUS

After being gone from the mansion for days, Antonius rushed downstairs to the door leading to the cell. Alice hadn't answered the phone in days and he was worried sick. Using his key, he tried several times to enter the heavily bolted door but all attempts ended in vain. It was also obvious that the locks had been changed.

"No! No! No!" He yelled banging on the door. "Alice, are you okay? Can you hear me?"

Silence.

His head leaned on the door as he continuously pounded on it with both fists. "Alice, talk to me! Please!"

Silence.

Antonius, realizing something was wrong stomped through the mansion until he approached Nine who was in the sitting room drinking wine. If he could've knocked her off her feet he would have.

Standing before her he looked as if he'd run a marathon, his face glistening from sweat. Taking a deep breath he said, "The door," he pointed behind him. "Is...is locked and I can't feed the prisoner."

Nine smiled. "The prisoner huh?"

He nodded.

"Sit down, Ian Greiner," she said, reminding him of his birth name. It was she who had given him the name Antonius as she did with every soldier who worked for her in the Legion.

"But the door is locked." He continued, wanting nothing more than to check on his precious love first. "Why...why did you change the locks? I don't understand."

"Don't make me ask again." Nine sighed. "These days I'm growing weary of the men I hold closely to my heart letting me down. And I won't stand for it anymore."

Antonius took a seat and wiped sweat from his brow. "Do you remember what you said to me when you were searching for Sheena some time back?"

"I said many things. I couldn't find my child and—"

"Do you remember what you said to me after I located her, in the motel room with a man much older than she?"

He searched his mind but it was truly difficult to recall. Because the only thing he wanted to know was why she changed the locks and if Alice was dead or alive. "No, I don't remember."

"Then allow me to tantalize your memory." She paused. "You said, *'I thought I lost her. And once again you came through for me.'*"

He shook his head having remembered. His mind now bombarded by thoughts of love for Alice and guilt of betraying the woman he pledged loyalty too. "I recall now." His breath slowed.

"Good." She nodded. "So now, having received back your memory, do you remember what I said next?"

He sat back. "You said that we are family. And that you reward loyalty with loyalty."

"Perfect, Antonius!" She clapped once. "Your memory is returning by the second." She smiled, crossing her brown sexy legs. "So tell me something what do you think I'd do with betrayal?" She glared.

He looked down, unable to look into her eyes. "I'm sorry, about—"

"What part are you sorry about?" She yelled, leaning forward. "Fucking my cousin, the woman you were supposed to watch? Whose sole mission in life is to take mine? Or promising your loyalty which at its very best is all a fucking lie!"

Silence.

"Remove yourself from my presence," Nine said softly. "You have broken my heart beyond repair."

Slowly Antonius rose and walked toward her. Standing in front of her he lowered himself and bent the knee. "I will never turn my back on you again." He kissed her hand, stood up and walked out.

NINE

Nine sat at the head of the table, Kelly to her right and no one to her left. Antonius, who had already lost five pounds from worry hung in the doorway, hands clutched in front of him like security. This would be an evening to remember, Nine was sure of it.

This meeting was mandatory with Bridget being the only one allowed to miss it. Solely because she alone handled the Prophet children and Nine realized she needed her to remain in that fashion.

The others, well, in her opinion they were all expendable.

Nine looked around the table at Lisa, Wagner, Jeremy, Porter, Isabel, Samantha, Bethany and Noel. "Things are going to be changing." Nine looked at them all with serious eyes. "And some of you may not like the new regime."

"What does that mean?" Lisa asked softly.

Nine nodded and stood up, walking slowly around the table. "Before the six of you arrived, you, your brothers, your son and your mother, I did things a certain way. And I'm sorry to say, but in my excitement for your arrival I abandoned my principals to appease." She paused and stopped behind Lisa, placing her hands on her shoulders as if she were about to break her neck. "And today that will stop."

"Did we do something wrong?" Lisa asked.

"Well you must have!" Noel blurted out. "Me, Samantha and Bethany don't even live here and now it feels like we're being put into some shit that has nothing to do with us."

"Be quiet, brother," Isabel said. "You sound ridiculous."

“Oh shut up crazy!” He responded.

“So you blaming us for this now?” Wagner asked Noel. “Before even finding out what’s going on?”

“I knew it,” Noel said to himself, shaking his head slowly from left to right. “I knew the moment we met ya’ll that something was going to go wrong. And now look.”

“You don’t even know what’s wrong yet,” Jeremy said, placing his prosthetic arm on the table. “Nine hasn’t finished telling us.”

“Listen, Onesie,” Noel continued referring to his arm, “if I know one thing since I been in this family it’s how to detect when something’s wrong. And I can tell before she even finishes that she’s all kinds of mad. And since me and my sisters ain’t been here—”

“It ain’t our fault you can’t stay here!” Wagner continued, his eye going too far to the left to be taken seriously. “Or that you lost that house you brought already because you don’t know how to handle your money!”

“SHUT UP!” Nine said slamming a fist on the table. Everyone settled and gave her their undivided attention. “My rules are simple. From here on out checks won’t go out just because we share the Prophet name. From this point on money will be distributed based on merit."

Noël's eyes widened. "Cousin, please don't do this. We just bought a new house and we're already behind. I—"

"Then you better get to work on what you need to do to be worthy."

Noel took a deep breath. "And I'm willing to do whatever I must," he said softly. "But, but how are we to be judged?"

"It's simple. Checks will be based on he or she who loves me the most and shows it." She sat in her seat, leaned back and smiled. "He or she who goes out their way to prove to me how much they want to be here." She paused. "How much they need me. I've given my love away for free far too long. Now it will cost you."

Antonius walked out while Kelly looked upon her daughter with extreme interest and approval. He knew this person talking was not Nine. Instead she was a woman put in place to divide Nine further from her family.

And yet he refused to say a word.

CHAPTER TWELVE

LEAF

"Neither a borrower nor a lender be."

- William Shakespeare

When Leaf made it to the house he rented he parked his silver Aston Martin in front, popped the trunk and removed one grocery bag and a bag of dog food. It was supposed to be a week but more time than that had passed. The neighborhood was miles away from the mansion he owned with Nine and not even a fraction of the cost but for him it felt more like home. Besides, too much was going on at Aristocrat Hills and he needed a breather.

He was almost inside his gate when he dropped the bag of dog food causing it to bust open and fall on the concrete. "Fuck!" He said to himself before placing the bag of groceries on the ground.

"I have it, I have it," a woman said who was gardening in the next house over. She grabbed a few things from her yard, opened her gate and ran toward him. The bottom of her feet black as soot. When he looked up her beauty astounded him. Her skin was pale, her hair fire engine red and her scent that of lavender. Wearing blue jeans shorts and a white top she was thin but still had a quiet sex appeal.

Using a trowel and bucket, she dropped to her knees and scooped up the dog food, tossing the remnants inside.

"Thanks, but I have it," he said stopping her by touching her hand.

"Nonsense," she responded, as she continued to scoop. "Besides, it's my pleasure."

Leaf remained standing and looked down at the woman as she went to work. When she was done she stood up, dropped the tiny shovel into the bucket and handed it to him. When he accepted she dusted her hands and extended one. "The name's Camille but my friends call me Red. What's yours, handsome?"

He shook her warm hand. "Leaf."

"Leaf like autumn huh?"

"Just like that," He responded, as that was his real name.

She smiled exposing all white teeth. "Now that's a name I could get used to saying."

"Is that right?" He picked up his grocery bag.

She nodded and smiled brighter. Looking behind her at her house she cleared her throat and said, "Well, I better be going." She ran her hands down her legs again. "Call on me if you need me."

"What if I'm calling now?"

She nodded and tried to stop her cheeks from showing her naughty intentions. His eyes said he wanted the full package. "I'd say let me make sure my husband's had his last pill and I'll meet you back over in fifteen." She nodded once, smiled and walked away.

Later, once he settled down, Leaf fed his dogs and watched them play happily in the yard. After reading several books on how to train animals he was amazed at how smart they were and how bad they wanted to learn. He taught them to answer on his command, fed them raw meat to keep them hungry and loved them like they were his children.

Leaf was a wealthy man so money was not a problem, which meant he could buy, do or go anywhere he pleased. But having the love of his animals made him feel somewhat complete, at least for the moment.

Truth be told Leaf was lost without Nine and even that word wasn't strong enough to describe how much he missed her. He thought about her constantly. He beat his dick incessantly thinking about the tone of her body and the way she smelled and felt.

But at the end of the day he was a man. A man who wanted particular qualities in his wife that lately Nine was falling short on. And until she fell in line, or unless she fell in line, he had every intention on fucking every bitch in America, be she black, white or brown.

An hour later Leaf was sitting on the sofa with Red on her knees, his black dick between her thin lips. The whole thing was this...even though he came ten minutes ago she still kept him in her mouth because she loved his taste.

"Bet your girl never sucked your dick this long before has she?"

He laughed and took a sip of beer.

"What's funny?" She asked, running her tongue around the helmet.

"My wife has fallen to sleep with my dick in her mouth at least fifty times that I can remember." He paused. "So yes, she has."

Red frowned, wiped her mouth and stood up, sitting next to him. Her bare ass on the sofa until he said, "Put that paper under you."

She lifted up, placed the front section of the Washington Post under her ass cheeks and plopped down, looking over at him. "If your wife is so grand, why this?" She crossed her arms over her tiny breasts.

He laughed once. "I could say the same about you. I mean, aren't you married?"

"My husband has dementia. I married old and rich." She exhaled. "And don't get me wrong but with him being 65 and me being 31 it just ain't the same in the bedroom. I do love him though but adventure calls me every now and again."

"And I'm adventure?"

"Aren't you?" She said.

He smiled. "My wife has too much going on right now at our house." He drank more beer. "But I have all faith this will make her come around."

"Meaning?"

He took a deep breath. "I ain't never do nothing like this before. Leave our home. Never even thought of cheating on her either. And I'm sure I'll have something to tell her when we decide to keep it one hundred with each other and get back together. But right now she needs to know that I expect a certain thing from her and she has to give it to me or else."

"Wow," she said. "You sound confident it will work."

"I am."

"Well, has she reached out yet? At least tried to be whatever vision you have for her?"

"Yes."

"So what happened?"

Leaf looked at her for a moment and put the can on the table. He wasn't the type of dude to trust everybody but she was not a part of his world so he felt safe. This was a woman who passed time planting trees and flowers, while fucking a nigga or two in the old fashion American way. He was a man who was brought up in an incestuous family worth millions, courtesy of the drug business. They were simply total opposites.

So who cared if he got real with her or not?

"She did reach out. Wanted me to love her and go with whatever plan she had for our future."

"And what happened?"

"I rejected it."

She laughed.

“Fuck so funny?”

“Sounds like you have a situation where your ego is clashing against hers.” She paused. “I don’t know how old you are but in my thirty-one years on earth I never seen a relationship end well that starts that way.”

“I’m in my early twenties.” He paused. “And maybe you haven’t lived an interesting enough life.”

“Could be.” She shrugged. “But all I’m going to say is you should prepare for the worst.” She got up and put on her clothes. “Good night. I hope to taste you again soon.” She winked and walked out.

CHAPTER THIRTEEN

LISA

"The better part of valor is discretion"
- William Shakespeare

Lisa walked down the corridor toward her room after rubbing Nine's feet for an hour. She was stressed after hearing the heartbreaking story of Maganda, Issa, Ori, Serwa, Lumo and Kessie, a group of women from Africa who escaped from a hair-braiding salon after being taken from their country in an act of modern day slavery. Led to America under false hopes by their cousin Fashna, Nine was devastated and immediately took them in.

In the end she allowed them to live in her home, on the west corridor, to flee from their captors. The women stayed out the way and since their arrival no one hardly ever saw them, because the refugees didn't want to be a burden.

It was definitely a Nefarious act.

Just like every other family member, Lisa was confused by what was demanded of her after Nine announced that they would be paid based on merit. In her heart she loved her niece and wanted to do right by her but this new attitude was scary.

When Lisa pushed through her room's door, she was shocked to see Wagner holding her son in a wrapped sheet by an open window. Placing her hand over her chest she desperately tried to slow her breath to prevent from passing out. "What, what are you doing?" She asked white palms in his direction.

"Stop right there!" He demanded. "Or I will see if he can fly."

Lisa could barely breathe and her vision started to blur. "Okay, okay what did I do? What got you so mad at me that you would do something like this, Wagner?" She said tearing up. "Because whatever I did I'm so sorry. It was never intentional."

"I think you had something to do with Nine changing all of a sudden."

"What?" She said with wide eyes. "Why would you think that? I don't have a relationship with her. She doesn't even like me."

"You lying!" He said moving closer to the window. "You told her that we planned to take the estate and now—"

"That's not true!" She extended both palms. "I don't know what made her act like this."

"You're a liar!" He moved closer to the window.

"Okay, okay, yes. It's true. I wanted to be closer to Nine but I didn't tell her anything. I promise."

"So she doesn't know about Kelly's plot to take over?" He asked, with clenched teeth.

"If she does it wasn't because of me, brother." She cried. "I promise you." She placed her hands on her chest. "Please, put down our son."

"Okay." He looked at her and smiled, before moving toward the window and letting go.

"NOOOOO!" Lisa ran toward the window and almost jumped out until Wagner snatched her and grabbed her to the floor while laughing hysterically.

"Calm down!" He continued to chuckle.

"Get off me!" She yelled fighting and pushing. "Let me go! You fucking killed my baby! You killed him!"

He angrily stood up, yanked her by the hair and forced her to look out of the open window. When she did she saw a life size doll on the ground below, it's limbs broken. "I was just fucking around."

She snatched away from him, even though he held a huge section of her hair in his hand. “Why…why would you do that?” She pointed at the window. “Why, Wagner?”

“So that you can remember who I am.” He moved closer and dropped the hair on the floor. “So that you remember what I can do if I find out you betrayed me.”

“But he’s your son.”

“Fuck that little nigga,” Wagner continued. “Like I said everybody been saying it’s a possibility that he’s our father’s anyway. You even named him after him.”

“I never slept with daddy!”

“It doesn’t matter! People around here thinking it.” He walked closer. “So if you know what’s good for you, you better keep what we discussed private. Or I’ma really drop you and that little nigga on your heads.” He smiled with rolling eyes, before walking away.

ANTONIUS

Antonius was lying face up in bed when there was a knock at his door. He got up, opened it and shook his head when he saw who was there. "What you doing in here?"

Lisa walked inside and closed the door behind her. "I wanted to say I'm sorry."

Antonius shook his head and sat on the edge of the bed. He rubbed his scraggly beard, not shaped neatly like it had been in the past. "For what?"

"For coming at you like I did. When you were trying to help me."

He sighed. "Even if I cared, which I don't, why you telling me this now?"

"Because I need help." She paused. "My brother, my son's father, may try to hurt my son."

"So go to Nine." He paused. "I'm nobody's hero anymore."

"She doesn't care about anything or anyone right now." She sat next to him and he got up, leaning against the door. "At least that's the way it seemed." Lisa took a second to examine him because he appeared miserable. "Wait, you look heart broken. You're in love."

He shook his head and wiped his hand down his face again. "You don't know what you talking about."

"I'm a woman. Of age and mind. And I can tell a man who's in love when I see one."

"Listen, your problem ain't mine. And my being in love has nothing to do with it."

"And I get that." She walked over to him. "I'm just asking you to help me, if the time comes and you can. That's all." She hugged him, let go and walked out.

CHAPTER FOURTEEN

NINE

"Ill wind which blows no man to good."

- William Shakespeare

Awake in bed, Nine lie face up, allowing the cool breeze from the open windows to soothe her. Leaf had been on her mind in ways she wished she could understand but every time she tried to think of him as if he was still hers, something told her in her spirit it was over.

Then there were the young women who stayed on the opposite corridor who had been enslaved. She appreciated that although she gave them help they let her be by staying out of her way. She also learned that they were undercover killers, something she could always use and would when the time was right.

KNOCK. KNOCK. KNOCK.

Nine sat up in bed and fingered her soft curly hair to make sure she was presentable. "Enter."

Jeremy came inside and stood in the doorway holding a guitar. "Good morning, my queen." He smiled brightly. "I wondered if I could sing a song for you. I heard you were having a bad day and—"

"Sure," she grinned. "What did I do to deserve this pleasure?" She asked while knowing that everybody in that bitch wanted to do what was necessary to keep those checks flowing.

Noel himself had just brought her breakfast; Bethany had offered to do everything short of eating her pussy, eventually settling on massaging her scalp instead. And Bridget stopped by with the kids who danced for her in a homemade skit. So yes, she knew what he wanted, a paycheck but at the moment any attention was better than none.

"I would like to sing to you because you deserve it." Jeremy lied his red face off.

She nodded. "Proceed."

The moment he opened his mouth Nine was taken aback by his voice. The words floated off his tongue so effortlessly that she wondered why she never knew his hidden talent existed. But it didn't matter. Only the present. So she allowed the soothing base in his voice and the way he controlled his tone to transport her to a better time.

His voice reminded her that she was a woman.

A woman in love.

She was just about to ask for an encore when, “Please get out of here with all that mess.”

Jeremy and Nine looked at who was in the doorway and they both shook their heads. It was Isabel dressed in the habit, which stunk to high heaven because she refused to take it off, believing that if she did she wouldn’t be able to stay sane.

“But I was singing for my niece,” Jeremy said.

“And your time is up,” Isabel said. “You sound like undercover trash anyway.”

He frowned. “But Nine liked—”

“It’s okay, Jeremy,” Nine said softly. “I’ll see you later.

Jeremy shook his head and pushed passed Isabel who walked into the room, locking the door behind herself. “Are you enjoying this shit?”

“What you talking about now?”

“You’re making a fool of yourself!” Isabel continued, tossing a card she held in her hand on the table next to Nine. “I want you to read that later.”

“Izzy, what do you want? Because you are extremely annoying at the moment and before you came I was actually relaxed.”

"Just stop it, Nine!" She yelled louder walking over to the bed and sitting down. "This person is not you. I mean, what are you doing?

Nine fingered her curly hair, crawled further on the bed and pulled the sheets over her chest. "Minding my business. Trying to relax."

"Then why have you been in bed all day?" She paused. "And who are those strange women in the west corridor?"

"Friends. And I'm in bed because I'm coming down with a cold."

"Because you're making a fool of yourself." She paused. "And...and I think it's something else too."

Nine fluffed the covers, looked at her and rolled her eyes. "Like what?"

"I know about Alice who lives under the stairs."

Nine rotated her head quickly toward her. "What you talking about?"

"I thought you killed her, Nine." She whispered.

"I did...I mean...I was going to."

"So why did I find your soldier fucking her then?" She paused. "Tell me that."

Nine waved her hand. "I don't know why it matters what I do to Alice. Everything that is going on she deserves."

"This is true," Isabel paused. "But what about him? I walked passed Antonius in the hallway earlier. He was apologizing to Alice even though she wasn't there. He looks so broken."

"Izzy, why are you so concerned with things that have nothing to do with you? Concern yourself with washing that habit. You smell like a bag of severed dicks."

"Because this is my home too."

"It isn't." Nine yelled. "You are a guest who has forgotten that at any moment I can pull the plug on all this shit."

"And guess what, I don't care."

"What does that mean?" Nine glared.

"If you don't want me here, put me the fuck out."

"You know you don't mean that, Isabel. First of all you begged me to stay when you were in the institution. Second of all if you aren't living here, where will you go? With your broke mother?"

Isabel stood in the middle of the floor trembling. "If only you knew what the voices in my head that are telling me to do evil things to you are saying."

"Isabel, get out of my face."

"No!" Isabel continued. "If you want me gone say it and I will walk out. But I'm not about to kiss your ass just because you have money and I don't."

"I'm warning you," Nine continued.

"If you want me gone say the word and I will leave forever."

Silence.

Seconds clicked by when Nine finally said, "Izzy, just leave my room." It was definitely obvious that the last person on earth she wanted gone, for whatever reason, was Isabel. Her brutal honesty was comforting in a house full of the kiss asses that she created. "I'm tired of talking to you and you're giving me a headache." Isabel was about to walk out when Nine said, "Oh yeah, please keep the fact that Alice is alive between you and me."

"You never have to ask me something like that. My lips are sealed," Isabel walked out.

KELLY

Kelly walked into her bedroom and locked the door when she saw Jeremy and Wagner waiting for her inside. "Where is your mother?" She whispered. "And your sister?"

"They not with it," Wagner said. "They said Isabel said to steer clear of you. But we are here so what's up?"

Kelly was seeing black she was so mad at Isabel.

"What about Porter?"

"He too busy following behind Isabel to listen to us," Wagner said. "So he not with it either."

Kelly frowned and flopped on the edge of her bed. Her plan included everybody. "But we need more. Because what I'm doing has to be permanent. I don't want our work to be undone allowing Nine to take the estate back."

"But why would it be undone?" Wagner asked, his eyes rolling around as always.

"You weren't there when our siblings tried to pull Nine off of the empire." She said. "Their fuck up is the reason she's still here."

"I wasn't in the initial meeting but we were there," Wagner corrected her.

"Yeah, it was because of us she was able to keep control of the money." Jeremy added. "Apparently with us being blood Prophets she needed our vote."

Kelly frowned. "Well the reason they messed up is because they didn't have Nine's ear. I do. We are working from the inside which means we have more control."

"What's the plan?"

"I will make her feel things and believe things. She'll go crazy thinking the world is against her. And when I'm done, and she's insane, no man, lawyer or judge will be able to believe she's capable of taking care of herself, let alone a multimillion dollar wine company."

"But most of the money is in drugs right?" Jeremy asked.

"Which she keeps cleaned up through real estate and that wine venture," she corrected him.

Wagner sighed. "You haven't told us what you want us to do yet."

"I'm going to dig into her head a little more. And I need to separate her from Isabel who right now is her only ally and getting on my fucking nerves." She sighed. "When the time comes I will need you to back me up. I'll leave it at that for now."

"What about the African girls in the west corridor?"

"What about them?" She shrugged. "They aren't Prophets. Once we gain control we'll throw them out on their black asses."

"Ain't you a little too sneaky for doing all this shit?" Wagner asked.

"I'm a lot of sneaky. So what do you think that'll make me do if someone betrays me?"

"Hey, as long as I'm getting my cut, I don't care what you got going on." Wagner said.

"I'm with him," Jeremy added.

"Well say no more brothers," she said.

KELLY

"Isabel isn't necessary for anything but getting on your nerves, "Kelly said as she combed Nine's short curly hair in front of her vanity mirror. "Can't you see she should go?"

"She is necessary to me."

Kelly sighed. "What possible worth can she possess?"

Nine took a deep breath, got up and walked to the bar in her room. "Isabel has always been a handful. This much is true. And she's gotten me into more trouble with Leaf than I care to admit. But...but with her at least I know where she's coming from." She opened the olive jar for her martini.

"And I don't tell you the truth?" Kelly asked with raised eyebrows.

"It's different." She poured vodka into a martini glass.

"Why?"

"Because I expect this of you, mother." She picked a few olives out and dropped them into the glass. "I'm your child. But with Isabel it's like...she doesn't want anything. Just for me to love her."

"News flash, Nine, everybody wants something." Kelly took a deep breath and sat on

Nine's bed. "Since you're so interested in the unpopular conversations I'd like to tell you something."

"And what's that?"

"I believe I saw Isabel sucking Leaf's dick before he left."

Nine dropped the martini glass and it crashed to the floor. "What?" She placed her hand over her heart. "That, that can't be true."

"I'm telling you what I believe I saw."

Nine walked from behind the bar. "If that were true...if that were true...why are you just telling me this now?" She glared down at her.

"Look how hard it was for me to get you to get this house in line. Look how hard it was for me to get you to understand that you were losing your husband and probably the estate too. And then you wanted me to add an infidelity into the mix? Sorry, Chocolate, but you couldn't handle it."

"Mother, I don't know about this," Nine said walking toward her kneeling at her feet. She placed her head on Kelly's knee and Kelly stroked her hair softly. "Izzy is...is precious to me. I can't understand or even believe that she would betray me like that." She paused. "First of all Leaf hates her and second of all, I don't believe it's in her makeup. I mean you said you *believe* and not *know* so maybe you're wrong."

Kelly frowned. "Maybe you're right." She paused. It would be harder to separate her from Izzy than she thought. "But there's something."

Nine looked up at her. "What is it?"

"She told me something else," Kelly took a deep breath. "She told me that Alice is still alive and that you are keeping her under the house."

Nine stood up and backed up into the wall. Now she knew she was telling the truth. First of all Alice was alive and second of all she just asked Isabel not to tell a soul. So why did her mother know? "But...but... why...would she tell you that. Why would—"

"It doesn't matter why!" Kelly yelled walking over to her. "It doesn't matter why anybody does anything. All that matters is what you do next. Get rid of Isabel. Now!"

Huge tears rolled down her cheek. "I need...I need my husband. I need him to help me get my mind clear because—"

"You don't need him!" Kelly turned Nine's face so that she was looking into her eyes. "All you need is me. And I'm here."

"But...but I..."

"Listen, my child, there comes a time in a woman's life when she must react. You may not like that Isabel has to go but you need to make an example out of her." She paused. "Today is as good a time as any don't you think?"

CHAPTER FIFTEEN

LEAF

Faith, and I'll send him packing."

- William Shakespeare

Leaf pulled up at a gas station with one of his dogs in the front seat growling crazily at everything that came near the car. After parking and putting in the pump, he walked up to the window, tapped it and smiled at the large puppy hopping happily inside. "I know you want some raw meat, my nig." Leaf said. "I got you when we—"

"Leaf," someone said calling behind him.

Leaf reached for the gun in his waist but relaxed when he looked at Aiden one of the soldiers in the Legion. "Oh my, God!" Leaf said dapping him. "How you been? I ain't seen you since that—"

"Bitch stabbed me," he said. "But yeah, I'm, I'm fine," Aiden stuttered. "I ended up divorcing her." He sighed. "But look, can you talk?"

Leaf looked at his car and back at Aiden. "Sure, why not?"

"Somewhere private?"

Leaf thought about it for a moment and shrugged. "Yeah, I gotta feed my dogs at home. So follow me back to the house. We can rap there." When they made it to Leaf's he gave Aiden a beer while they sat in the living room on the sofa. "So what's up?"

"I need your help with something that's confidential."

Leaf nodded. "If I can I will."

Aiden took a deep breath and sat his beer down on the floor. "A friend of mine had, well, he kinda had this relationship with a person and now that person is blackmailing him and he doesn't know what to do."

Leaf smiled and shook his head.

"What is it?" Aiden asked.

"Listen, if you want my help you gotta be honest, otherwise you're wasting my time and I got shit to do."

Aiden nodded and took a deep breath. "Okay, I...I kinda experimented with this guy and—"

"Experimented?" Leaf sat his beer down. "I'm confused." He clutched his hands in front of him.

"I let him...suck my dick."

Leaf frowned. “I…I’m sorry I reacted like that it’s just, I ain’t with that gay shit if you trying to come on to me.”

He shook his hands. “No, no, I didn’t mean it like that,” Aiden continued. “And I definitely wouldn’t come at you.”

“I’m shocked I can’t lie.” Leaf picked up his beer and took a large sip. “Didn’t think you rocked that way.”

Aiden wiped his hand down his face. “This is bad I know but—”

“It’s not that it’s bad I just, I guess I just need for you to tell me what you want from me.”

Aiden downed all of his beer and put the can down. “I need some help in finding this dude.”

“Why?”

“Because if word gets out that I’m gay, like he threatened to tell the city, then it may cause problems with my friends and my work with Nine.”

Leaf laughed. “I don’t know about all that.” He guzzled all of his beer and opened another. “I’m talking about your business with Nine being ruined.”

"Yes it will." Aiden scooted closer, causing Leaf to scoot backward. "I heard she killed one soldier for the same thing."

"Aiden, I know my wife and one thing she won't do is kill you for your sexual preference." Besides, the Prophets were the last people to point fingers with all the shit they had going on. "So if you heard that then you wrong."

Aiden sighed and looked down. "Maybe you right."

"I know I'm right."

"Well maybe I didn't know her the way I thought. And because I get a lot of money with you and Nine and...well...with her new dude Antonius and all I—"

"Fuck you just say?" Leaf placed his beer down. "What you talking about her new dude?"

Aiden moved uneasily. "I was saying that...um...never mind."

"I asked you a fucking question." He asked through tight teeth.

Aiden shrugged. "I figured since Antonius and Nine were together now and you living here I probably should've gone to them instead. But I don't know Antonius like that either."

“Did you see them together?” Leaf glared, his nostrils flaring.

“Nah. But I know he hasn’t been to his house in almost a week so I figured they were together.”

“You know what, get yah shit and get out, bruh.” Leaf stood up and looked down at him.

“But I—”

“Bounce, nigga!”

Aiden stood up and rushed toward the door as Leaf followed. He was about to close the door when Aiden walked away. But Red stepped into the fence. She looked at Aiden speeding off and walked up his steps. “Everything okay?”

“Long story.”

“Well you feel like company?” She grinned.

Leaf shrugged and walked away, leaving the door open. Thirty minutes later, when the fucking was over, he lie in bed with her drinking beer. “You wanna talk now?” She said laying her head on his chest.

“Not really.”

“Why do I get the feeling that isn’t true?”

He took a deep breath. “I just found out someone I always believed may be fucking my wife actually is.”

She nodded. “So what you going to do?”

"Right now I'm trying to refrain from going over there and killing everybody but my sons."

She ran her finger down his chest. "Is it working?"

"Nah."

She stopped moving her finger and sat up, her back against the headboard. "What do you want?" She paused. "I mean really."

He looked up at her. "What does that mean?"

"Leaf, if you love your wife, why don't you do right by her and go to her? Instead of being in here fucking me?"

"For the record I didn't come to you. You came over here for the D."

"I know." She exhaled. "That's not what I'm saying but..." She took a deep breath. "It's obvious you moved here to get your wife mad. And it's also obvious you got a problem with her moving on with her life. So if you feel that way go to her."

Silence.

She shook her head. "So you gonna let her stay with the other man?"

"Let me be clear, even if I don't get my wife back the last thing I'm gonna do is let her rest easy with that nigga. Blood will pour."

"What does that mean?" She asked.

He said too much, which is why he preferred she bounced after their fucking session was over. "Maybe you should go home." He looked up at her.

"But we were—"

"I need to be by myself. Please don't let me ask again."

She snatched the sheet off the bed, wrapped it around her body and stormed into the bathroom.

CHAPTER SIXTEEN

NINE

"If he swagger, let him not come here."

- William Shakespeare

Nine sat in the living room drinking wine when Antonius walked up to her looking like death. She was wearing black stretch pants and a black Gucci zip hoodie as she had just finished jogging. Getting comfortable her polished red toes wiggled. "Antonius," she said taking a sip. "What can I do for you?"

"Nine, I'll be leaving."

Slowly she sat her wine glass on the table and walked over to him. Her heart thumping wildly. "Why?"

"Because I can't, I can't honor you the way you deserve." He sat on the sofa and she moved closer, sitting next to him.

Placing a hand on his knee she said, "What does that mean?"

"You know what it means, Nine. I...I need to know she's okay." He paused. "And...and I know this angers you but—"

"Wow." She removed her hand. "So it's true. You are in love with my cousin."

"Yes." He paused. "And I'm sorry but, it's been weeks and, and I need to know she's okay. And since I can't...I can't be here anymore. Knowing she's under this house longing for me."

Nine took a deep breath. "I'm losing everything I care about." A single tear rolled down her face. "Everything."

He turned toward her. "But you aren't. It's just that, people grow into different versions of themselves with time." He ran his hand down his face. "And my love for her will never change my love for you."

"But she's not a good person, Antonius."

"She used to be that way." He paused. "She told me about the things she did when you were here and..."

"And still you care about her?" She glared. "Despite the torture I endured?"

"And you got her back, Nine." He paused. "Plus I wouldn't care if I thought she was the same person." He paused. "But I'm telling you this woman is different. She has changed. You putting her in prison worked."

Nine walked away and flopped into the recliner. "If I were to show you her, if I were to let you see that she is alive, would you stay?"

He nodded. "Yes."

She took a deep breath. "Then come with me."

NINE

Nine opened the door were Alice was kept using the key she had hung around her neck. It was the only key and she kept it close to her bosom for protection. The moment the door pushed open, Antonius rushed inside and up to the bars.

"Alice," he said looking at her frail body. He couldn't tell if she was sleep or dead. "Alice, it's me. Are you okay?"

Slowly Alice's head rose off the bunk she was sleeping on. When her hair fell back from her face Antonius was disgusted at the bruises. He rushed toward Nine and shook her like a piñata. "What have you done?" He shook harder. "What have you done to her?"

"Does it matter?"

"Yes!" He said with baited breath. "Yes it does. I…I…"

"Let me go," Nine demanded. "Now!"

Slowly he released his hold and looked at the palm of his hands. "I'm sorry. I will…I will never touch you in that way again." He paused. "But she…she has been tortured. Why, Nine?"

"Don't blame her," Alice said in a low tone. "I did the same to her when…"

"Well I'm tired of hearing about the past," Antonius said marching up to the bars. "I'm tired of the excuses used to condone such barbaric behavior by both of you. I'm tired of it all!"

"What does that mean?" Nine asked, a tear rolling down her face. "Are you still going to leave me?"

"Are you going to let her go?" He asked with raised brows.

"I love you, Antonius, but I'm afraid that's something I will never do." Nine said plainly. "But if you break yet another promise, I will show you, through her, how far I'm willing to go to make you pay."

He shook his head. He couldn't believe the level of hate Nine had reached just to keep him under her thumb. "You really are a cold person."

"You may have your opinion," Nine said smoothly. "But I have your Alice."

He looked down and back at her. "I have always respected and loved you. But if you continue to do this to Alice, who I adore, I will leave you forever, Nine. And then you will truly be alone."

Nine walked closer enraged. "Will you stay or will I be forced to murder this bitch?" She was done with the dumb shit.

He lowered his head, shook it softly from left to right and smiled with hate. "I'm staying." He paused. "Now please leave."

Nine walked away and when she turned around to close the door she could've sworn she saw Alice grinning sinisterly. But her expression was now covered with Antonius' body so she couldn't be sure.

It didn't matter.

For now she had won.

NINE

Nine held Magnus to her chest as she rocked him quietly in his room. Although she had given birth to him she was amazed at how much of Leaf's features he'd already taken. Even his skin was yellow.

"I thought you would be enough," she said to herself. "Why aren't you? What is wrong with me?"

"Enough of what?" Bridget asked walking into the nursery.

Nine looked back at her and at the baby again. "Nothing." She took a deep breath. "You know, I really appreciate how great you are with the kids."

Bridget walked over to Kerrick II's bed and began to straighten the spreads. The children were in the playroom across from the nursery and Lisa was watching them. "Don't worry," Bridget said as she fixed the bottom sheet. "We're family." She paused. "Plus being around babies reminds me of when Jeremy was little."

"Jeremy? What about Porter and Wagner? They're triplets."

"I know but Jeremy was always so loving. Whenever I was sad he would wrap his arms around my neck and sing to me. Telling me everything would be okay. He sings to me everyday even now."

"I enjoy his voice too." Nine nodded. "And I also understand the love of a child. Julius brought me a lot of light before Magnus was born. He still does now."

Bridget smiled. "I wanted to talk to you about something."

Nine looked at her.

"I wanted to know if, well, if something were to happen to you, who would take over?"

Nine frowned. "That's an odd question."

"I know and I don't mean it that way but...I still must know." She paused. "Nothing means more to me these days than security."

Nine placed her baby in the bassinet and walked over to her. "Considering things are so odd right now, why would you ask me something like that? It gives me pause and makes me weary of you."

Bridget looked around. “I love it here.” She breathed deeply. “For the first time in my entire life I feel at home and, Nine, I had a terrible life.” She sighed. “Definitely nothing close to what you’ve gone through but still.”

“So don’t compare.”

“I’m sorry and it seems so disrespectful but I need to know if it’s okay to fall in love with this place. I need to know if it’s okay to tell my children to fall in love with being here also. And the only way to truly be safe is if we were to have some sort of written piece of paper that gives us a right.”

Nine frowned. “Are you asking for a percentage of the estate?”

“Why not?” Bridget shrugged. “I did give birth to Kerrick’s children. And it’s because of us you have the estate.”

“Which is why you should be grateful that she allowed you to stay here,” Kelly said entering the room and the conversation.

Bridget looked at Nine and cleared her throat. “Maybe we can talk later.” She nodded at Kelly and walked out.

“Can you believe that ungrateful bitch?” Kelly said.

Nine sat on the sofa in the room. "I actually respect her."

Kelly frowned. "And why is that?" She walked toward her.

"Because like Isabel, at least I know where she's coming from." Nine took a deep breath.

"Speaking of her, I see you allowed Isabel to remain." She paused. "Now you have another traitor on your hands with Bridget. In a minute it will be a mutiny."

"I don't see it that way. With everyone jabbing at my pockets from behind, Bridget's honesty, was, well, sort of refreshing."

"Well don't get too refreshed. Because before I entered I did hear something that made a lot of sense. If it is true that she gave birth to Kerrick's children, then they have as much right as me and your aunts and uncles."

"Right doesn't give you claim, mother."

"I know."

"So what is your point?"

"Just be aware, Nine. That's all."

Nine looked at her and smiled. "You know something, mother. Since you've been here Isabel says I've been tense and unhappy. Why do you think that is?"

Kelly looked at Nine before opening and closing her mouth.

Nine walked away.

KELLY

Kelly walked up behind Bridget and grabbed her arm. Bridget snatched away quickly.

“What do you want?” Bridget yelled.

“What are you going to do? Because if you don’t take my side now you won’t have a chance later. Trust me, it will be a big mistake to side against me.”

“Bitch, just stay away from me and my children. Isabel was right about you. You are the devil.” She stormed away.

KELLY

Growing agitated about Isabel's interference, Kelly crept into her room preparing to strangle the breath from her nostrils. When she made it there and pulled back the sheet her hands moved toward Isabel's neck until Isabel flipped a button on the knife she was holding and jumped on Kelly.

Knocking her to the floor she said, "I sleep with a blade at all times. How about you?"

"Get off me, Isabel," Kelly said, afraid to move because she was worried she'd be cut.

"Why shouldn't I kill you right now? You were about to kill me."

"I wasn't going to—"

"I want you to leave this house or I will tell Nine about all the secret meetings you've been having. I may not have any idea what you're talking about but I can guess and if that doesn't work lie." She paused. "If you don't leave, I promise, I will do the craziest performance ever and bring this blade across your neck. In time Nine will forgive me. Am I clear?"

CHAPTER SEVENTEEN

NINE

"I am a man more sinned against than sinning"
- William Shakespeare

Face up in bed; Nine had her eyes closed as Lisa sat at the top of the bed, her back against the headboard as she massaged her temples while Bethany rubbed her feet. She knew the reasons they were there, for the money, but it didn't matter. With Leaf gone she needed the attention to prevent from going mad.

Nine was about to drift off into sleep when Isabel stormed inside. "Why did Kelly order my things to be removed from the room?"

Nine looked at her and sighed. "Did you ask her?"

"She told me to ask you!" She walked closer.

"Lisa and Bethany, leave us please." When they were gone Nine said, "I want you out by the end of the day."

Isabel's eyes widened. "What for? Just because I choose not to buy into whatever shit you have going on here?"

"Because you tried to stab my mother in her sleep." Nine said. "She told me about it this morning."

Isabel's jaw dropped. "Me? That's a fucking lie! She was the one who walked into my room and tried to stab me."

"Oh, like you tried to stab Leaf that time? Which caused me to have to put you in an institution?"

"That was different! I was really off my meds. But this—"

"What about the fact that I told you not to tell anyone about Alice?" She paused. "And what do you go do? Turn around the same day and tell her what you saw."

"I didn't. She already knew because—"

"Save your breath."

Isabel moved closer and sat down. "I don't want to leave, Nine. "And it's not for the reasons you think. I'm not here for your money or anything like—"

"Isabel, you could not possibly know what I'm thinking." Nine said louder. "So stop and just leave."

"But you need me."

"Just get out, girl," Kelly said entering the room. "I have packed your little trinkets and your crusty panties and it's time to go now. I mean why are you pressing the situation? She doesn't want you here. How many times does she have to tell you that?"

Isabel looked at her aunt. "Why are you this way? You are her mother and you are so much more evil than you should be."

Kelly laughed. "You mean why am I smart enough to see that you are a snake? And that you never meant my daughter any good? Just go and stop wasting everybody's time."

Isabel looked at Nine again, tiring of Kelly. "I don't want to leave because you need me, Nine. And you may not be able to see that right now but you will when I'm gone. And I don't want that for you."

"She has me," Kelly said.

"And since you've been here she has lost her husband and her mind," Isabel said. "Which is odd because as far as I knew I was the craziest one around here."

Nine picked up the phone and made a call that was out of earshot of Isabel. Five minutes later Antonius walked in with two men. "Take her out of my house," Nine said. "Quickly."

"Nine, don't do this!" Isabel pleaded, tears welling up in her eyes. "You are all I have in this world and I don't deserve to be separated from you. Please, I'm begging you."

"It's too late for all that," Kelly said.

"She's gonna kill you," Isabel yelled as she was being taken out of the room by the two men. "She's going to kill you and take it all, Nine! Please open your eyes and look at what she's doing!"

When she was gone Kelly walked up to Nine and touched her hand. "I'm very proud of the woman you've become. And I know it's hard but you will get over her leaving with time." She hugged Nine and grinned sinisterly.

PORTER

After witnessing Isabel being thrown off the property and left at the opening of Aristocrat Hills, Porter drove up to her in his blue BMW and rolled the window down. "Where you going?"

"I don't know yet," she said pacing as she ran her hands down her face. "I don't wanna…I don't wanna hurt anybody but…but…Kelly makes me want to do awful things." She looked at him with wide eyes. "They want me to be this person but I don't want to be this person. I…I…I'm trying to keep my sanity."

Porter remembered being told how crazy she was by Leaf but now seeing it for himself he understood. So why couldn't he leave? And why wasn't he afraid? "Did you wanna get in until you figure it out?"

She looked around and took a deep breath before getting inside. "I don't like what's happening here. I think they are trying to hurt Nine."

"They?"

"Well, maybe just Kelly."

"I agree." Porter said driving off the property. "Before she came Nine was so cool and now..."

"She's still cool." Isabel leaned her head against the window. "And I miss her already."

"Yeah...she is cool," he said looking over at her trying to say whatever he could to get into them draws and her heart. "Well, not really, seeing as how she's treating you and all."

Isabel looked at him. "You don't know her to make that statement." She leaned her head sideways on the window. "We didn't have our mothers and, and I guess part of us still want them in our lives."

"That could be true but still." He continued to drive.

Isabel positioned herself so that she could look at him. "If you really like me, are you willing to prove it?"

He shrugged. "I don't see why not." He paused. "Leaf took the dogs and I ain't got shit else to do around here."

WAGNER

Jeremy and Wagner held pool sticks as they stood over the table in the basement of the mansion. All everybody could talk about was Isabel being escorted off the property like a bag of dog shit. "If she got rid of her then she won't have no problems throwing one of us out," Wagner said. "I heard they were close at one point."

"So what do we do?" Jeremy asked as he hit the ball, sending it flying toward the corner pocket.

"We have to get creative." He said slowly. "At least until Kelly comes up with the rest of her plan. Even though it seems to be taking forever."

"Well she did say she needed to get rid of the people around Nine. So maybe it is working. Isabel *is* gone," Jeremy said.

"Yeah, but in the meantime we have to stay on her good side in case Kelly fucks up."

Suddenly Jeremy began to smile. "I don't know about you but I'm gonna do the idea."

Wagner frowned. "What idea?"

Jeremy tossed the stick down and ran out of the room.

NINE

Nine stood in front of the mirror in her room with her cell phone against her ear. Taking a deep breath when she heard Leaf's voice she said, "I don't know where you are. I don't know why you left but...but I need you back home. Without your love I can't see my own reflection anymore. Please, Leaf. If you hate me say it. If you don't love me anymore...I...just come back and talk to me."

When she ended the call and put the cell phone down she heard notes from a guitar playing in the distance. But where was it coming from? When she moved toward her window she saw Jeremy standing on a ladder up against the house smiling. Opening the window she looked down at the deep drop below him. "What are you...what are you doing?"

“I wanted you to know how much I appreciate everything you’ve done for me. So I chose to serenade you from afar.” He paused. “Now please, sit down and allow me.”

Worried, but intrigued, she smiled, pulled up her vanity chair and said, “Proceed.”

Leaning on the ladder, he gripped his guitar with his replacement arm and began to sing, *You are so beautiful.* Nine smiled brightly as she listened to his melodious voice. Suddenly she closed her eyes and imagined it were Leaf who was singing to her and tears streamed down her face. In that moment she made a decision that she would go find him no matter where he was or what he was doing.

When she opened her eyes the song was over and Jeremy said, “I appreciate everything you have done for me and my family.”

“Thank you,” Nine said softly. “The pleasure is all—”

Suddenly the ladder jolted and Jeremy’s eyes widened. The guitar fell out of his grip as he snatched at the air to break his fall. It didn’t work. Nine extended her hand but he was already spinning out of control, a look of death upon his face.

"Jeremy, no!" Nine yelled just before he hit the ground, his head busting open like a melon.

Witnessing such terror, she backed up and fell to the floor. "NOOOOOOOOOO!"

CHAPTER EIGHTEEN

NINE

"Fie, foh, and fum, I smell the blood of a British man."

-William Shakespeare

Nine sat naked in her room, in a corner, surrounded by complete darkness on the floor. The blackness provided her with comfort as she spent most of her life under that very house going over her thoughts the same way. The funeral was earlier that day and she was wrecked with guilt. And there wasn't a scenario she could reach where the ordeal was not her fault.

There was a knock at the door.

Although she gave no permission it opened and Antonius came inside. Turning on the lamp he grabbed a red sheet off the bed and walked over to her. After covering her body he lifted her up and sat her on the bed.

Nine crawled in a ball and broke down crying.

"This isn't your fault," he said softly rubbing her back. "Don't put this on yourself."

"But if it hadn't been for me—"

"Nine, this isn't your fault." He repeated. "You didn't suggest that Jeremy climb on a ladder and sing to you from a window. He was a grown man who made a bad decision and it caused him his life. But I'm not going to let you blame yourself."

She looked up at him, her eyes red from crying all night. Her short curly hair lying close to her face from sweating. "What is happening to me?"

"Too many people."

"What do you mean?" She sat up and wrapped her body with the sheet.

He took a deep breath. "Nine, you are beautiful. You are strong. But you are also very wealthy. And wealthy women breed leeches of the worst kind." He paused. "And what you need right now is support."

She shook her head and looked down. "But I don't have that anymore. My husband is gone."

"Where is he?"

She took a deep breath and wrapped herself tighter in the sheet. Antonius tried to look away but everything about her was perfect, despite his love for Alice. "I don't know, Antonius. I wish I did."

He nodded. "Well you should find him."

"I can't chase a man who doesn't love me." She sighed. "And he's made that painfully obvious by leaving."

"Don't talk like that," he said.

She got up and walked toward the window, before staring down at the land. "Antonius, do you...hate me?" She looked at him and he walked toward her. The moonlight lit both of their faces.

"Never."

"Despite?"

He took a deep breath. "I don't understand a lot about this family, Nine. So I stopped judging it a long time ago." He paused. "What I do know is that I could never hate you even when I tried. And trust me, after what I saw with Alice I did try."

She nodded. "What makes you...what makes you love her?"

He took a deep breath and ran his hand down his face. "She listens. She's beautiful and maybe even her...despair is attractive to me."

"You like women in despair?"

He shrugged. "I prefer my women happy. But a sad woman is vulnerable and in a world so fake, vulnerability is refreshing."

She smiled. "Do you really believe that she's genuine?"

"I don't know because I never, *ever* felt like this." Nine nodded, a tear running down her cheek. He wiped it away with his thumb and kissed the same spot. "What I feel for her will never take the place of what I feel for you. They are polar opposites and completely different."

"But what does that mean?"

"It means I could never have you in the way that you will allow me. And I'm not talking about sexual gratification. I'm talking totally. Even if we ran away today I would always know that I'm a placemat for your one and only love."

"Leaf." She sighed.

"Leaf," he repeated.

She looked out the window. "What can I do that would make you happy?" She asked softly.

"You don't have to do anything for me."

"I know. But still I'm asking."

"Nothing, Nine. I want nothing from you. Just your peace in all of this madness."

When she looked into his eyes she could tell he was being sincere. "I'm going to free Alice."

His eyes widened and his jaw dropped. Because prior to that moment he never thought freeing her was an option or else he would've asked immediately. Besides she said she would never free her repeatedly. "Nine, I love you, but if this is a cruel trick I can't take it."

"I wouldn't hurt you like that, Antonius. You don't deserve it."

"Are you...are you sure?"

She placed her hand on his cheek. "Yes."

"But I thought because of the history that...you know."

"And I still feel that way, Antonius. But I also trust you. So if you're telling me that by letting my sworn enemy out I will remain safe, and you will be happy, that's what I want. I'm doing this for you."

He ran his hand down his face, his breath quick and heavy. "But...but..."

"It's okay, Antonius." She held his hand. "You don't have to say anything because I know how you feel."

"Nine, you don't realize what this means to me." A tear rolled down his face. In all of the years she'd seen Antonius he never cried. "You don't understand what..."

She looked out the window. "I just want some of the pain to stop in this house." She shook her head after seeing a flash of Jeremy's lifeless body in her mind. "I caused a lot of hurt over the past few months and I have to figure out a lot of things. And quick. But the last thing I want is you worrying or unhappy with me."

He pulled her toward him and her sheet dropped. His body heated up and stiffened. He'd never been that close to her nakedness and slowly he let her go and turned around. "I'm sorry."

She picked the sheet up and hid herself. "I'm covered."

He turned around and took a deep breath. "I have always admired and cared about you but today...today it's reached an entirely different level." He stepped closer. "And I will never, ever, forget what you've done for me, Nine."

"I know, Antonius." She smiled. "I know."

CHAPTER NINETEEN

KELLY

"Double, double toil and trouble, fire burn, and cauldron bubble."

- William Shakespeare

Kelly walked into Bridget's bedroom where she was consoling her children Porter, Wagner and Lisa who were distraught after having to bury their brother. They were all sitting on the bed in misery.

"I said it before but I must say it again," Kelly started. "I am so sorry for your loss," She said.

"This is the second worst day of my life," Bridget whispered. "And to be honest I don't know how I will cope without Jeremy."

"The second worst day?" Kelly asked. "What was the other?"

"When Kerrick died."

Kelly nodded. "Father meant a lot to me too." She closed and locked the door. "He meant a lot to a lot of people in this family who are being ignored financially."

"What you want?" Porter asked growing agitated with her greed. There was no hiding the fact that he didn't care for her. As far as he was concerned she was starting unnecessary trouble and he wanted her dismissed. "We not trying to hear nothing about Nine right now."

"You know why I'm here," Kelly glared. And took a deep breath. "I mean don't you agree now that she must pay for what happened to Jeremy?"

Bridget shook her head. "I just lost my child and yet here you are throwing yours under the bus. And trying to kill her."

"Never said kill," Kelly corrected her.

"But why do I feel it's your ultimate goal?"

"You're a snake," Lisa said to Kelly. "And I don't trust you."

"You have your opinion."

"I do. And it won't change."

"Let's hear her out," Wagner said to his siblings and mother. "I mean we might as well."

"I have nothing to say to her," Lisa said standing up.

"Why do you even like her?" Kelly asked. "She hates you."

"And still she takes care of me," Lisa responded. "I'm not going to stab her in the back like this." She paused and looked at all of them. "And when things fall down you better hope you are on the right side because I know I will be." She stormed out.

"I'm going after her," Porter said leaving too.

Kelly looked at Wagner and Bridget. "So what do you both think?"

"I think right now all I wanna do is grieve over my child," Bridget said as she wiped tears away.

"But we don't have a lot of time for all that," Kelly persisted.

"She's right, mother," Wagner said.

Bridget looked at him. "You can't possibly feel that way."

"Ma, can't you see things are already changing around here? You said yourself you were worried about our security; maybe Kelly is how we secure what's coming to us. Kerrick was my father and yet his granddaughter is running the estate? What type of shit is that?"

"I don't know," Bridget said. "But this is wrong."

"This is my final offer." Kelly said. "I won't ask you again. However Lisa was right about one thing. Now is the time to choose a side." She pointed at the floor. "Now Jeremy died filling an unreasonable request by my daughter. And all I wanna do is help my siblings get where we need to be."

"And where is that?" Bridget asked.

"At the top of the Prophet empire," Kelly said. "And don't worry once I'm at the helm I will be fair."

"What's the plan?" Bridget asked.

"We go to the police."

"The police?" Wagner yelled. "That's your fucking plan?"

Kelly was growing frustrated with the bunch. "Why do you act like you aren't due millions?"

Wagner sighed. "It's not that. I just didn't think you meant we'd get outsiders involved."

"It's the only way," Kelly said.

"Not really." Wagner replied.

Kelly looked at him closely and crossed her arms over her chest. "I'm listening. What's your plan?"

"We kill her for real," he said.

Kelly's eyebrows rose. "Now look who's willing to go the extra mile."

"If we kill her we could run things from the inside," he continued. "We could maintain control from the beginning and nobody would have to know."

"But she doesn't have a will."

"If they find out then we would end up having to fight it out with other family members," he shrugged. "At least we would still receive large portions instead of small bits."

"But I want it all." Kelly said. "Not only that, you have no idea how greedy our sisters and brothers can be. They would find a judge to say you aren't due anything because you are illegitimate and they would win." She paused. "But if we go to the police and stick to the story that she pushed Jeremy out the window, as a criminal she will not be allowed to maintain access to the estate. So that means me with the will I created."

"You don't want to kill her but it's not because you are her mother," Bridget said. "You want her alive to suffer again."

Silence.

Wagner folded his arms over his chest. "I think you underestimate Nine."

"How would you know?" Kelly frowned. "You just came along all of some years ago."

"And that's why it's easier for me to see." He ran his hand down his face. "Something says she won't go out like this. I mean, she's fucked up now but I don't think she'll stay down forever."

Kelly nodded and paced. "I guess we will see." She walked out.

"She may be our only way but something tells me she's still trouble." Wagner said to his mother. "Plus I heard she be peeing all over the mansion."

"That's not her," Bridget said. "It was me."

He stepped back from her grossed out and embarrassed. "But why?"

"I was marking my territory."

His jaw dropped and he closed the door and locked it. It had been a long time since she'd been on medication for her psychosis and he thought that part of their lives was over. Now he knew he was wrong.

"Ma, maybe we should up the meds don't you think?"

"I know you think I'm crazy but this house belongs to you, Porter and Lisa. We have every right to be here. Maybe it is time to take it."

LISA

"Porter, you don't understand because you were always chasing females out in the street, leaving Wagner to direct his hate on me." She sat on the edge of the bed in her room. "He's different when we are alone. The kind of different that chills the soul."

"What does that mean?" He asked.

"He's...abusive. To me and little Kerrick."

His eyebrows rose. "Why you never said anything before?"

"Because mom tried to keep us together and I didn't want her to know the hate that was going on behind closed doors. Plus sometimes Jeremy was involved and you know how much she loved him."

"And what that mean?" He yelled. "You should be tortured?" He cracked his knuckles. "I'm about to fuck this nigga up. He messing with nephew and—"

"No!" She yelled stopping him. "Please don't do anything. Just...just let it go. Trust me, he will get his due. I prayed on it."

"So I'm not supposed to say anything to him either?" He asked pointing to himself.

Silence.

"This is crazy." Porter continued running his hand over his scalp. "What is going on with this family?"

"I know it's hard but please leave it alone. I'm begging you. Let me handle it. Because if you hurt him he won't just hurt me. He'll go after my son too."

Porter sighed. "Okay. For now." He dropped his hand. "But if I detect anything foul I'm going at him hard."

He stormed out.

CHAPTER TWENTY

ANTONIUS

"Come what come may."

- William Shakespeare

Antonius was headed to the basement when he heard Lisa crying in her bedroom. His heart wanted to free Alice first but something about Lisa's sorrow demanded his immediate attention. "Are you okay?" He asked standing in the doorway.

She nodded yes.

"Then why are you crying?" He paused. "Is he messing with you again?" He frowned.

"No it's a combination of everything."

He placed his hand over his face as if he finally understood what was happening. "Please forgive me." He dropped his hand at his side. "I've lost so many niggas in my life that sometimes it makes me insensitive to death and I totally forgot. That you just buried your brother."

"It's okay." She sniffled, wiped her tears and looked at him. "You seem different though. Why?"

He nodded. "Well, I have some good news."

"Share."

"I don't want to with Jeremy being gone and—"

"If there is anything that I need right now it's good news." He looked at her and walked deeper into the room, closing the door behind himself. "The woman you saw in the cell, well, she's gonna be free."

Silence.

He was surprised at her non-chalant attitude. "What is it?" He asked. "I would think you'd want a prisoner to be free."

"I don't know what to feel really." She placed her feet on the bed yoga style. "I mean, it makes me wonder what other horrible things Alice did to get put there in the first place. I remember her vaguely and the feeling wasn't good."

He frowned. "Wow."

"I don't mean to be cruel and I don't know Nine well at all. I actually have been trying to get close to her but nothing seems to work." She sighed and looked down at her fingers. "But I do believe if she put her there, in that cell, for as long as she did, there has to be some reason and that you should be careful."

He cleared his throat. "You know what, you let me worry about her. You just take care of yourself." He moved toward the door and stormed out.

ANTONIUS

Antonius walked down the steps along the hallway and up to the room that held Alice. When he entered she was inside sitting on the floor along the wall within her cell. "You shouldn't be back, Antonius. I thought we agreed the last time would be the last time." She paused. "I can't keep seeing you out there knowing you will never be mine."

He smiled and opened the cell door. Walking up to her he extended his hand.

She looked at it. "Antonius, please go away."

"Take my hand, Alice. It's over. It's all over."

Her eyes widened. "What do you mean?" She grabbed his hand and stood up.

"Nine has had a change of heart."

She covered her mouth with her hand. "But I don't understand…I…I."

"You're free." His smile grew more intense, filled with excitement. "You're fucking free!"

She wrapped her arms around his neck and screamed. "Oh my, God! Thank you! Thank you!"

ALICE

Alice sat in the passenger seat of his black BMW looking at the cars, land and structures they passed by as they drove away from Aristocrat Hills. Relishing in the feeling, Antonius placed his hand on her yellow thigh and smiled. "How you doing over there?"

"I thought I would die there."

"I was starting to worry about that too." He sighed and eased on the beltway. "But I underestimated how much she cares about me. And for that I'm grateful."

Alice turned toward him. "She's in love with you. After all of these years how did you never touch her when you clearly had the chance?"

"In love with me," he said holding his mouth open. "Not even close, Alice. She's not thinking about me."

"Then why else would she be crazy enough, some would say even stupid, to let me go?" She looked at him intensely.

"People change, Alice."

"Do they?" She asked firmly.

He looked at her. "I certainly hope so."

She took a deep breath, blinked a few times and looked away. "Forgive me, Antonius. I, I just never thought she would care enough to release me. Thought I would rot in that place forever."

"Let the past stay where it is, Alice. It has more use there. All I want now is to get you home and take care of you."

"Take care of me," she repeated allowing the words to float off her lips. "Even at my best no one cared enough to take care of me. I'm...I'm so grateful for you. You're my hero."

"You deserve this."

"Yes. I do." She smiled brighter. "And so much more."

ANTONIUS

Antonius looked at Alice as she lay napping peacefully in bed. She had already been bathed twice, since the first bath left water so grungy inside the tub she couldn't get properly clean. And now after nursing her wounds, feeding and making love to her, he watched as she slept.

Slowly she opened her eyes and stirred a little when she saw him gazing at her. "Wow, it's real." She stretched her arms out on the bed and rubbed the smooth 800 thread count sheets. "I'm in heaven. I'm really in heaven." She paused. "Please tell me I'm not dreaming."

He grinned. "Definitely not a dream."

She sat up and looked around the room. Everything was elegant with the color theme being black and opal, which was very masculine and fit him perfectly. "You saved me," she said reaching out for him. He softly grabbed her hand, sat on the bed and pulled her into his arms. "Will you continue to love me?"

"Forever, Alice."

"Over anybody?"

He looked at her. "Over everybody."

CHAPTER TWENTY-ONE

KELLY

"You shall hear. As good luck would have it, comes in one Mistress Page."

- William Shakespeare

Kelly, Bridget and Wagner sat in a detective's office in the police department waiting to give more details on their claim. That they had information on a murder. While Kelly was ready to throw her child under the bus and back up twice, Bridget was still nervous and apprehensive.

Kelly seeing this looked over at Bridget and smiled. "You know, my mama had the most beautiful hair. And the most perfect tone of white skin you'd ever seen."

Bridget sighed. "Yeah, I saw a picture of her before from Kerrick." She looked away, preferring not to imagine even in death Kerrick being with another woman.

Kelly took a deep breath. "Victoria Fole was her maiden name," she continued reminiscing while looking at the walls. "Anyway, I would stare at her blonde hair forever and her eyes were like brown candy."

Wagner saw his mother getting uncomfortable and sighed deeply. "You mind telling me the point of all this shit?"

"For all of her beauty, my mother was also extremely weak." She sighed, ignoring him. "Leaving daddy room to find many women and even allowing one of his whores, whom my child grew to love, live in our house." She glared at Bridget.

"What really happened to her?" Bridget asked. "Your mother."

"She died of a broken heart a little after daddy did. All because daddy chose Nine over her to run the Prophet fortune."

Bridget sighed. "I get what you're trying to say, Kelly."

Kelly rotated toward her quickly. "Do you?" She paused. "Because right now it looks like you don't." Her teeth clenched tightly together. "Now Nine has killed your boy and the least you could do is toughen the fuck up and get your revenge. That estate belongs to your children and me. Let's take it!"

"Sorry I took so long," a tall slender white man with pale skin said walking into the room. "I'm detective Larry Novak." He took a seat. "How can I help?" He scooted closer to the table and for some reason they all liked him.

Kelly looked at Bridget and Wagner and took a deep breath. "Like I was telling the other officer, we came to report a murder."

He removed a small pad from his pocket along with a blue pen. "Who was the victim?"

"My son." Bridget said softly.

"His name?"

"Jeremy."

The detective continued to write and they couldn't figure out if he believed them or not. Finally he looked up from scribbling and smiled at each one of them. "Sorry to hear about this. I really am. Death of a child is always hard." He cleared his throat. "So when did this occur?"

"A little over a week ago." Kelly said.

"Okay," the detective took a deep breath and leaned back into his chair, causing it to squeak. "How?"

"First I wanna say that the perpetrator is my daughter." Kelly informed.

The detective's eyes widened. "Is that right?"

"Yes." She clutched her hands on the table in front of her. "So it hurts me to come here today."

"Does it really?"

She frowned. "Yes. Of course. What mother would want to turn her child in for something so horrible?"

He leaned forward. "That's what I want to find out."

"My daughter," Kelly cleared her throat. "Was recently given a lot of money and it has gone to her head in ways you can't imagine. You have to understand. She wasn't used to anything so valuable and it has made her, well, evil." She paused. "Besides, most of her life she had one dress and one night gown. How could she possibly be able to handle millions?"

Wagner and Bridget looked at one another surprised at the news.

"Wait, didn't you say she was given money?" The detective questioned as he continued to write.

"Yes...uh..."

"And you said she is your daughter correct?"

"Yes, but I—"

"Well did you come from meager beginnings too?"

"No." Kelly looked down at her hands.

He was confused. “Well did your child stay with her father? Who perhaps was poor?”

“No. We both lived together.” Kelly wiped a strand of long black hair behind her ear. Refraining of course from telling him that Nine was the product of incest between brother and sister.

“So why was this daughter being given so little when you clearly had so much?”

Kelly moved uneasily in her seat and tried to squeeze her ass cheeks together to prevent from farting. She prepared over and over in her mind the questions she thought he would ask in the hopes of leading the investigation. But now it became painfully obvious that she looked like a fool.

“Ma’am.” The detective said. “Please answer me.”

“My child,” she cleared her throat. “Well she had problems.”

“What kind of problems?”

“Mental ones. And as a result we had to keep her away from others.”

“So you and her father resorted to self medication?”

“You don’t understand!” Kelly yelled.

His eyes widened. “Well that’s your problem not mine. You see, you are here to convince me of a crime. A major one against your daughter at that. And for me to believe you I must have background information to support this claim.”

Kelly took a deep breath. Possessing a troubled mind herself, which is why Kerrick committed her to a mental institution, she was becoming unraveled. “My daughter was violent.”

“Did you put her in an institution to get this diagnosis at least?”

“No.”

“Well why not?”

“We had to do things our way.”

He smiled. “Your way huh?”

“Yes. The Prophet way.”

He frowned and leaned forward. “Wait, what is her name?” His hand shook.

“Nine Prophet,” Kelly said feeling as if it all were lost. It was obvious the man didn’t fuck with her.

He dropped the pen and it rolled to the floor. “Nine Prophet? Whose family was involved in that incest scandal last year?”

“That was all disproved after it was discovered that the woman had broken into our home and tried to kill us," Bridget said knowing the case full well.

"No, it was disproved after your family tossed money around." He paused. "I was involved with that case and almost lost my job behind it. Oh yeah, I definitely am interested now." He picked up his pen from the floor. "Give me everything you have on this woman. And I do mean everything."

Kelly, Wagner and Bridget smiled.

CHAPTER TWENTY-TWO

ANTONIUS

"Look on me well: I have eat no meat these five days."

- William Shakespeare

Antonius drove down the street with Aiden and when they came upon a brick building he pointed out the window. "It's here."

Antonius looked in the backseat at his two men and nodded. After Aiden gave them some additional information they exited and moved toward the building.

"Thank you for helping me with this," Aiden said. "I didn't know what else to do."

Antonius sat back in his seat and sighed. "I think you need to make a decision."

"On what?"

"On what you wanna be." He said seriously. "If you a gay man do your thing and stop getting other people involved. Because all this is a bit much."

"But I'm not gay!" Aiden pleaded.

"I said if…you…are…a…gay…man," Antonius said slowly. "You need to open up to it instead of coming at niggas for help. It's strange and a total misuse of my time. Especially with everything I have on my plate."

Aiden looked down. "I know. And I'm sorry. I just…I just…"

"Don't worry about it now," Antonius sighed. He could see the turmoil in his eyes. "It's done. My men gonna make sure whatever he does in his life talking about you won't be it."

"At least you didn't do what Leaf did."

Antonius looked at him quickly. "You went to Leaf?"

"Yeah," he sighed. "But he didn't seem happy to see me. I mean you aren't either but he definitely wasn't. Put me out his house and everything." He paused. "Especially after I mentioned you and Nine."

Antonius leaned toward him. "Come again."

"I told him I didn't wanna bother him and that I wanted to ask you for help but I figured you were busy even though you have always been kind to me."

Antonius shook his head. "For someone who doesn't want people thinking he's gay you sure telling the world about it." Antonius paused. "But what does this have to do with me and Nine again?"

"I just mentioned that you two were together and—"

Antonius eyebrows lowered. "You told Leaf we were together?"

"Yes."

"But why when it's a fucking lie?" He slapped his hand on his face. "No wonder this nigga hates me."

"I just thought—"

"I want you to take me to where he lives. Tonight!"

ANTONIUS

Antonius pulled up later that evening in front of Leaf's house. He dropped off Aiden and the two men who had beaten the blackmailer senseless earlier and was ready to get down to other matters.

The moment Leaf saw his face he gritted his teeth. "Hold up." He told him. The dogs were barking crazily so Leaf directed his attention to his animals and the white woman sitting on his porch drinking peach tea. After he put the dogs in the backyard he walked up to her and said, "I'll see you later."

"Later it is." She winked, got up and walked barefoot to her house next door.

Antonius entered the gate, closing it behind himself. "What you doing, man?" He pointed to the woman. "You really putting it all on the line? Out in the open? The last thing you want is Nine rolling up around here on you."

Leaf laughed.

"Why you posted up with that bitch when you got a wife at home?"

"I have a wife?" He pointed to himself. "Because from what I'm told she belongs to you now." Leaf said with a glare.

"Well that's a lie."

Leaf laughed and Antonius took inventory of how grungy he looked. Not to mention that months of drinking incessantly had started to darken his yellow skin, greying out the features that once made him handsome.

"You a fool," Antonius said.

"Excuse me?" Leaf glared.

"You have the woman of my dreams and you throwing her away."

"So you finally being honest?" Leaf's nostrils flared as he took one step closer.

"I have never lied to you, you just didn't ask the right questions. Nine and I remain platonic but at one point I would have given the world to be with her. And you out here looking a fucking—"

Leaf stole him in the face and followed it up with a gut punch. "I just put my gun up," Leaf said pointing at him. "And that makes you one lucky nigga."

Antonius held his bleeding mouth. "If it wasn't for Alice she'd be mine." He still said no matter how mad he was.

Leaf's eyes widened. "Alice?"

"Yeah." Antonius walked to the gate and out of it, leaving it wide open. "So I consider *you* to be one lucky nigga."

"Nine let her go?"

Antonius stopped walking. "Yeah. And I can tell by the look in your eyes you're surprised she freed her." He looked at the blood on his fingers.

"Maybe you don't know the woman you supposed to care about as much as you thought you did. But I do."

"Be careful with my cousin." Leaf said. "She's dangerous."

"Like you care."

"I don't."

Antonius smiled. "You know what, let me tend to mine and Nine." He looked across the way at the woman who stepped back out her house. "And you worry about your white bird." He got into the car and shook his head.

Once the door was closed he opened the glove compartment snatched a few pieces of tissue out and wiped his bloody mouth. Afterwards he took a deep breath removed his phone from his pocket and called his house.

Alice moaned before she answered. "My love, is that you?" She yawned.

"It is."

"I'm so sorry about sleeping so much. It's—"

"Don't apologize. You've been through a lot." Antonius may have been casual over the phone but his mind was definitely on what Leaf said about Alice. Was she the one for him? Or was she really evil? "I love you."

"I love you more my dear, Antonius. Come home to me. I miss you already."

"Say no more."

CHAPTER TWENTY-THREE

NINE

"Some are born great, some achieve greatness, and some have greatness thrust upon 'em."

- William Shakespeare

Nine walked down the hallway toward her bedroom naked. A bottle of wine in one hand a glass in the other. When she pushed her door open she was surprised to find Leaf standing in the middle of the floor holding a brown paper bag. "Leaf," she said nearly breathless. "I..."

"Come in. And close the door."

She walked inside and pushed the door closed softly with her foot before sitting the wine and glass on the bed table.

"I went to the West Corridor and saw you have more people here. Women from Africa."

"Yes," she cleared her throat. "They were enslaved, forced to braid hair at a salon. So—"

"You helped them."

Silence.

"What are you doing here, Leaf?" She asked. She didn't feel like talking about what went on in their house. He had lost his privileges.

He smirked, put the bag on the bed and walked toward the bottle of Merlot, pouring himself a heaping glass. As if he hadn't drank in days he guzzled it all and poured another handing the glass to her.

"I live here," he said. "Remember?"

"I know but..." She put the glass down and walking to the closet she grabbed a robe.

"Don't cover yourself." He said softly. "I wanna look at you."

She dropped the red velvet robe and it fell softly at her feet, her back still in his direction. His eyes rolled down the slide of her neck that dipped right at the top of her ass. She was a work of art.

"Leaf, please don't," she said softly, turning around. "Don't do this to me. I thought it was over. Please don't mess with my mind. I can't take it."

"All I wanted was you," he said. "Ever. It's like the moment I saw your face I knew you were for me." He walked toward the bed and picked up the bag handing it to her.

"What is this?" She asked.

"Open it."

She did so and smiled when she pulled out a honey bun. She was given little food when she was a hostage in the house and the honey bun was the first treat he'd given her. She immediately was transported back to the first time she'd eaten one when they were falling in love. "Thank you."

He winked, took it out her hand and put it on the table by the wine. Taking a deep breath he said, "Do you want me?" His sentence barely above a whisper. As if hearing the words outside and fearing her answer would cause him to die.

"More than I ever wanted a person, place or thing."

"But how can you be sure?"

"Because I have said your name to myself for every hour you've been gone."

He nodded and smiled.

"And now you are here," she continued. "Standing before me. And all I can hope and pray is God, please let him be here forever."

He moved closer and took her hand softly. "I have no doubt that you are a very powerful woman."

"Leaf, I—"

"Shhhhh...just let me talk. I have no doubt that you are powerful but you are not alone, Nine. You can't make decisions and then treat me like an after thought. I can't stand for it anymore."

"So what do you want?" She asked. "For me to leave our home?"

"Would you?"

"What are you asking me, Leaf?" She said firmer. "Whatever it is be a man and say it."

He sat on the side of the bed and pulled her toward him with a small tug of her hand. As she stood between his legs he kissed her bare belly. She smelled of coconut. "I don't know what I'm saying right now. What I do know is that it can't continue like this. I'm losing my patience and feeling violent without you."

"Jeremy died."

His eyes widened as he looked up at her. "What? When?"

"It's a long story but after that happened guilt and loneliness had me rethinking a lot of things. Maybe I did wrong by you. Maybe our breakup is our fault."

"Loneliness?" Leaf said. She said many things but his mind was still on petty mode. "Are you really?"

She frowned and took one step back. "What's that supposed to mean?"

"You know."

"Leaf, what are you talking about?"

He laughed, irritating her even more.

"Leaf, what do you mean?" She said louder.

"Antonius."

"What about him?"

"When are you going to admit that you had a thing with that nigga?"

"Never because it's not true."

He laughed and stood up. "Yeah, okay."

"Leaf, why would you come back if you don't believe me?" She threw her arms up. "It's obvious that all you wanna do is fight so you can have an excuse to walk out. If that's the case don't create a tale at my expense. Just go." She pointed at the door.

"You would like that wouldn't you?"

Nine grabbed her robe and slipped it on. She took a deep breath and smiled. It hung open wide showing the glow of her body. "You come here dipped in the funk of a white whore and disrespect me?"

"White...white whore?" Leaf felt his body jolt. How had she known?

She laughed.

"What are you talking about?" He yelled as he ran up to her and touched her shoulder.

She slapped him off like a fly. "Get the fuck off me!"

He released her and walked away. "If we are going to work—"

"Leaf, it's over."

"You don't mean that."

"Why don't I?" She paused. "I have done all I could to show you how much I love and want you back, even at the expense of myself and my feelings. I never did more begging in my life!" She yelled. "I even allowed you to carry on with that bitch knowing she could never amount to me or stand in my shoes."

He laughed. "So he told you?" He asked referring to Antonius.

"Who told me what?"

He realized in that moment that maybe Antonius hadn't said a word and just like always Nine was on her job. "I'm gonna leave for awhile to give you some time to rethink all of this, Nine. And when you realize who I am you will return. I'm sure."

"You know, Leaf, when you left I didn't understand who I would be without you. I never, ever, envisioned my life without you. But it's amazing how clear my mind has been over the last few weeks. It's almost like I'm feeling more like myself than ever. Maybe I'm purging." She paused. "Go away, Leaf. And when you get home you'll find something cold and wet waiting for you in your bed, courtesy of me. Enjoy."

CHAPTER TWENTY-FOUR

ANTONIUS

"To hell with you and the whole pack of you who triumph at my misery."

- William Shakespeare

Antonius and Alice sat at the dining room table with Sheena, his daughter, eating spaghetti and garlic bread that she made.

Alice grabbed her fork and ate another bite, savoring the taste. "Sheena, this is really, really good." Alice nodded. "How did you learn to cook so well?"

Sheena rolled her eyes.

Alice looked over at Antonius and dropped her head, which enraged him beyond belief because her feelings were hurt. "Sheena!" He yelled. "Have some respect for our guest! She was giving you a compliment."

"Why?" Sheena yelled dropping her fork on the floor. "Just for her?" She pointed at Alice. "Because she's related to your precious, Nine Prophet?"

"It's okay." Alice said wiping her mouth with the white linen napkin in her lap. "Maybe I should go to the room and eat my food." She moved to leave when he softly pulled her hand.

"No, don't go," he said before looking back at Sheena. "Apologize to her now."

"I'd rather eat her pussy instead. And as nasty as she left the tub that would be something wouldn't it?" She got up and stormed out of the kitchen and then the house.

He shook his head and looked at Alice. "Listen, I am so sorry about her behavior. She hasn't been right since her...well...maybe I should leave it alone."

"No," Alice said placing a hand over his. "Tell me."

He took a deep breath. "Awhile back Sheena had been missing for some time and it drove me insane. Her mother hasn't been in the picture for years and I have sole custody and it's been very, very difficult." He took another deep breath. "Anyway it turned out that she had run away with Mo Wright, one of Nine's men."

"Wow." Alice said loving the tea he was pouring.

"Yeah, it was very, very hard, especially since she was underage and I didn't see the time."

"The time?" She repeated.

"The time necessary for them to get to know each other. I didn't see him with her and I didn't even know she knew anybody from our business but she did."

"Well what happened? How did you get Sheena back?"

"I asked for Nine's help. She was able to catch up with her and—"

"You know, sometimes I feel like I will always be competing with her. It's like she's this myth that is always out of reach. What if it happens again? And Sheena runs away. I don't have the power to help you."

"But I don't want your help. I want you as my woman."

"Where is my place in your heart, Antonius? Huh? Where is the place in your heart that's exclusively for me? Because right now it feels like it's shared."

"Alice, what do you mean?"

She took a deep breath, got up from the table and walked away. Bare feet slapping against the hardwood floor. Worried, Antonius followed her to their room. Once inside he closed and locked the door and leaned against it. "What do you want from me?" He said softly. "Tell me so I can offer it to you. So you can know how I feel."

"I want you."

"Well you have me, Alice."

"But it doesn't feel that way."

He pulled himself off the door and walked toward her. She was frustrating him because he wanted to prove he cared. "Listen to me."

"No."

"Listen," he said gently. "Nine is a friend and nothing more. You don't have to compete with her because there's no reason."

"Does she know that?"

"Nine, isn't thinking about me."

She frowned. "That's not a good answer and why do you keep saying that shit? It sounds like if she was *thinking about you*, you would leave me in a heartbeat."

"Alice—"

She flopped on the bed. "Just stop it."

He sat next to her and put his hand over hers. Then he slid to his knee and opened the drawer next to him, removing a gold ring box. "I was gonna—"

"Oh my, God," she said covering her mouth when she saw the diamond inside.

He gently pushed her hands down to her lap. "I was gonna do this on the weekend over dinner, outside of the house, but I want you to know how I feel now." He took a deep breath. "When I found you in that cell I was confused because I didn't know what was happening. Or why. But as years passed and I spent more time with you, alone in the darkness, I saw your inner beauty as well as your outer."

"Antonius, I..." tears rolled down her cheek as she trembled.

"Alice Prophet, I guess what I'm saying is this, will you do me the privilege of being my wife?"

She wrapped her arms around his neck and nodded her head up and down as she cried harder.

He laughed softly. "I'm gonna need an answer, baby. Don't leave me hanging."

She released him, gripped his face in her hands and kissed him. "Yes! Yes! I will be your wife. Of course I will!"

They stood up and embraced.

"And, I want a quick wedding too," she said wiping the tears from her face roughly, leaving red bruises along the way. "I don't need nothing big or fancy. Maybe I'll invite some of my cousins though, I don't know yet." She was so giddy she could hardly keep still.

"I'll marry you tomorrow if you desire," he slid the ring on her finger and tossed the box.

"Yes, yes, please!"

Antonius grabbed her hands and looked into her eyes. Slowly he removed her clothes and stared at her body with great appreciation and love. He was no longer gazing at his girlfriend's body but his fiancé's. And when she was undressed he undressed himself.

Totally naked, he lifted her up and immediately inserted his stiffness inside her warmth. Carrying her to the bed, still connected to her, he pushed inside of her again.

Her head flew back into the pillow. "I love you so much," she whispered as she kissed him, suckling a little on his bottom lip. "Sometimes I feel like you're a dream."

Softly he pumped into her. "You mean everything to me." He said wiping her hair out of her face so that he could look into her eyes. "Everything. Always."

"Do I?" She whispered.

"Yes. Everything."

"Then prove it to me."

"Anything you want."

"Kill Nine."

"Wha...what?" The breath had been knocked from his body upon hearing her words. It was as if he was dropped kicked and had fallen from the tenth floor out a window. "What are you talking—"

"I want her dead," she said as she continued to pump into him harder to capture his mind and body with each thrust. "I can't have her in the world knowing what she did to me. For two years I endured abuse. I mean, I got her the one time but look at what she did to me. She went way overboard." She frowned. "And I can't have her in the world knowing that she loves you as much as she does." She paused. "Killing her would be the only way I will be your wife."

He continued to move inside her body but this time extra slow. Feeling a tingling sensation his head fell in the cup of her neck and he inhaled her Jasmine perfume. "I love you so much," he said.

"I love you too, Antonius."

He raised his head and looked down into her eyes as he moved even slower, huge tears dripping on her face. “I have never felt this way about another woman. And I’m sure I never will.”

“You don’t have to,” she responded pumping harder. “We have each other.”

Suddenly he moaned filling her up with his cream. In a heavy breath he rubbed her face before his hands traced alongside her neck. “I’m so sorry, Alice. But you won’t hurt Nine.”

He squeezed. Hard. He applied all the energy he could muster to take her breath away. She clawed at his face, leaving scratches as witnesses but he didn’t stop until she was dead and the love of his life gone. Taking with her his hopes and dreams for the future.

Rolling off at her he looked up at the ceiling and screamed, “WWHHHHHHHHHHYYYYYY?!!!!!!!”

CHAPTER TWENTY-FIVE

NINE

"Thus bad begins and worse remains behind."

- William Shakespeare

Nine stood in the middle of the living room dressed in tight black leather pants and a grey silk button down blouse, a diamond necklace anchored her neckline. Bethany, Samantha and Noel were behind her while Kelly, Bridget, Wagner and Lisa stood in front of her. Porter, although in the house somewhere, missed the meeting because as usual no one truly knew his whereabouts.

The refugees who lived with her had been sent to do work for the drug empire and as a result were gone for the week.

"Leaf is no longer welcome in my home," Nine said firmly.

There were a few gasps but Nine, as regal as ever, remained strong. Unmoved by the confidence and beauty she was born with.

"Is there anything I can do?" Lisa asked. "To make things easier for you? Maybe contact your men and make sure security is beefed up in the meantime?"

"You just tend to your son." Bethany said with an attitude. "Me and my sister got everything else. Trust and believe."

Lisa nodded. "Sure, I...I just wanted to be helpful since we all live here."

"That was rude," Bridget said to Bethany. "That's your aunt you're talking to by the way."

"Excuse me?" Bethany responded.

"You are grandchildren but Lisa is Kerrick's daughter and that makes her your aunt, deserving of a little more fucking respect. Besides she has just as much right to this place as you do!"

"It doesn't matter," Nine said. "Grandfather left all things to me and that means I rule. Now I have been fair in—"

"Fair!" Bridget yelled, her craziness oozing over the room. "So you think it's fair that I lost my son due to your egotistical behavior?" She was so angry she was trembling because she held her feelings in for so long. "You know what, Nine, I had such hope for us when we first got here and now I see that it was all a facade."

Nine laughed.

"What is so funny?" Bridget yelled.

"Greed." Nine said.

"What does that mean?"

"It's amazing how contagious it can be. Your son died and the first thing you talk about is money?"

KNOCK. KNOCK. KNOCK.

"I'll get it," Bethany said. She walked toward the door as detective Novak and four men appeared on the other side. Confused, everyone crowded in to see who was visiting.

Nine stepped in front of them all. "Who are you?" Nine asked before frowning. "And how did you get on the property?"

Detective Novak flashed his badge. "I am here for you, Nine Prophet. You are being arrested for the murder of Jeremy Prophet."

Nine's eyes widened. "What for? I mean why? It was an accident! Ask anyone!"

"We will ask all our questions downtown." The men with the detective moved to Nine's right and left and held her firmly.

"But I didn't kill anyone! Jeremy's death was an accident." She pleaded. "Let me go."

"We will talk about all that at the precinct."

Nine looked at Kelly. "Mother, please help me!" The two men continued to hold her. "Tell these men that I didn't harm Jeremy. Tell them it was an accident."

Kelly laughed hysterically before she slowly quieted. "You have been a thorn in my uterus since the day I gave birth to your black ass," she said with hate raging through her veins. "And I don't know what you did to father to make him choose you, but it's over now, and I want you out of this house!"

"Mother, please!" Nine cried. "Why are you saying these things to me?"

"Take her away!" Kelly said. "I'm tired of looking at her."

They gripped Nine firmly and rushed her toward the door.

"Now," Kelly said turning her back to Nine while addressing the pack. "I am in charge." She raised a sheet of paper she made up. "I found father's will and this document, which is official, clearly states that I will rule. This is a new day so everyone of you had better—"

Suddenly there was laughter. Heavy and yet pain ridden it still sucked the confidence out of Kelly's speech.

Slowly Kelly turned around to see Nine standing before the men who at first held her so tightly. "What's going on?" Kelly asked them. "Take her away."

"I finally get it," Nine said walking slowly toward Kelly. "I finally see you for what you truly are. Or maybe I knew it all along but it hurt too much to come to terms with. That Isabel was always right."

Kelly trembled. "And...and what exactly do you see?"

"That you hate me. And that you will never love me."

Kelly swallowed the lump in her throat.

Nine slapped her on the left of her face and then the right. "You disgust me. Your lying ass doesn't even have cancer. I checked, mother."

Kelly, realizing that once again she'd been outwitted dropped to her knees. It was painfully obvious that she was taken for a ride, which would ultimately lead to her fate.

"I told you not to side with her," Lisa whispered to Wagner who was trembling.

Nine looked behind her at the men. "Take her downstairs to the cell." With the surprise over it was now obvious that although the men were dressed in all black, none of them had badges. That's because they weren't officers at all. Instead they were men of Nine's Legion.

On Nine's order they lifted Kelly to her feet with her crying for mercy all the way.

Only one man remained behind.

When she was gone Nine walked up to Detective Novak. "Are you sure she was alone when she tried to report this lie to the police?"

Wagner attempted to hide in the crowd by taking one step back.

"She was alone," he said. On the take, the officer decided to go for self. He had been on Nine's bad side before and almost lost everything. This time he moved by the old adage. *If you can't beat 'em, get paid by 'em instead.*

"Are you certain?" Nine repeated.

"I sure am." He looked at Bridget and Wagner who looked away. Nine had paid him $75,000 for the information on her mother but he had plans to extort them too, later. "It was clear that Kelly was going to put the crime all on you. And—"

BOOM!

Suddenly Nine's soldier who remained shot the detective in the back of the head. With his body at her black Prada heels, Nine slowly raised her head and looked upon her family.

"I don't do snakes. Of any kind." She walked over to Bridget and took a deep breath. "I respect you." Nine said, hands clutched in front of her. "You have always told me where you are coming from, no matter how painful. It takes a big woman to do that. With that said, you and your family are no longer welcome in my home. And I want you out by week's end."

"So there's nothing I can say to get you to change your mind?" Bridget asked. "We have no place to—"

"My decision is final."

"But the greatest leaders compromise."

Nine laughed. "It is through compromise that you are still alive," Nine corrected her. "Because your eyes tell me that if you could do more to me right now you would."

Bridget nodded and walked away with Wagner and Lisa following.

Nine looked at her family and the body on the floor. "I remember a time when I had nothing. I was abused simply because I reminded grandfather of the love he could no longer have with the only woman who truly ever had his heart in Africa." She paused. "And although he begged for my forgiveness, by giving me all, money has also shown me an even darker side to people," she took a deep breath, "An even darker side to myself."

"Sometimes having everything is worse than having nothing at all." She paused. "And yet it is my cross to bear and I carry it proudly. But know this." She eyed them all. "I always, and I do mean always, think five steps ahead in every war. While you all have had the world given to you I was left alone with nothing but the knowledge of books on how to win to keep me company." She looked down at the detective's body. "You could never outwit me. So don't even try." She smiled, held her head up and walked away.

CHAPTER TWENTY-SIX

LEAF

"O beware, my lord, of jealousy; It is
the green-eyed monster which doth mock the
meat it feeds on."

- William Shakespeare

Exhausted, Leaf pulled up in front of his house and parked his ride. After talking to Nine he decided to stay at the Four Seasons a few days to clear his head and still he hadn't gotten a wink of sleep. At the end of the day he loved her more than he was willing to admit but in self-discovery he realized something else about their relationship too.

In the beginning he had fallen in love with the meek young woman who lived under the house while never learning to love the infamous Nine Prophet. The two women were definitely opposite although both loved him deeply.

Pushing out the door he walked toward his house and could hear his dogs barking crazily. He sighed. "I'm sorry guys," Leaf said as he removed the key from his pocket and unlocked the door. "I know you're hungry."

"Your animals been going at it all night!" A neighbor with pale white skin yelled outside of his gate. "Very rude!"

"I got it now." He said walking into the house shaking his head.

The moment he entered he smelled an odor so foul it rocked him. Covering his nose he moved toward his bedroom coughing a few times. The heat being on blast made it worse and he was certain he didn't turn it on before he left. Besides, it was spring. Somebody wanted the smell to stink to high heaven and it did.

Removing his .45 from his pocket, he walked further and kicked the door open with his foot.

Aiming inside he was shocked when he saw Red lying on the bed naked, her throat slit open. Putting his gun down on the dresser he backed against the wall.

"Nine," he whispered.

Red walked through the open front door of Leaf's house as she was instructed in a text message from his number. Hornier than a school of fourteen year old boys, she was excited about the possibilities. "Leaf," she said seductively hoping to get a little dick before feeding her husband his daily meds. "Where are you?"

But when she made it to the bedroom she wanted to run back out when she saw Nine sitting on the bed elegantly dressed in all white, legs crossed calmly. There were five beautiful women also present, dipped in black tights and black hoodies. They were the refugees, Maganda, Ori, Serwa, Lumo and Kessie.

Maganda locked the door and stood in front of the exit, preventing Red from leaving.

"I...I know you," Red said to Nine. "I saw you the day—"

"You met with one of my employees and agreed to stop fucking my husband."

Ashamed, Red looked at Maganda. She remembered her clearly because before Maganda approached her she saw her across the room and said Maganda had to be the most beautiful woman she'd ever seen.

"Yes, she did tell me to stop and I didn't," Red said. "I'm so sorry. It's just that Leaf made it sound like it was over. I even tried to tell him to go to you and fight for his relationship but he seemed so, so angry. And I—"

"Loved fucking him."

Red nodded. "Yes. I did."

Nine stood up and removed her white high heels with the red bottoms one by one. "I can't lie, I can see how it would've been hard not fucking my cousin. He knows how to work that thing." She removed her dress to prevent blood from splashing on her.

"Your cousin?" Red repeated. But I thought you were together."

"That part too." Nine winked. "Trust me. It's complicated."

Red was confused but there was no time to investigate or elaborate on the Prophet incestuous ways. "Please, don't hurt me."

"I'm afraid it's too late for that part." Nine walked toward her red Hermes bag that sat on the bed and removed a large serrated knife.

Seeing the blade, Red was about to scream until Maganda's hand came slamming down over her mouth.

Nine stepped toward her. "You kept him from me longer than need be. And at this time your pussy will no longer be needed." Slowly she brought the knife across her neck, the sound coming from her flesh similar to slicing a ripe orange.

When she was dead Nine sighed. "Your move, Leaf." She said to herself as she watched her body hit the floor.

PRESENT DAY

NINE

Nine walked into the kitchen where Isabel was sitting drinking coffee as if Nine hadn't told her to kick rocks weeks ago. She was still wearing the habit, which at this point desperately needed to be cleaned.

Instead of being mad, Nine shook her head, walked to the counter and poured herself a cup of coffee. "So you no longer pretending to be gone huh?" Nine asked sitting across from her.

Isabel picked up her red cup and took a sip. "I told you my purpose was to save you. So I paid you no mind and just did my thing."

"I knew you were still here, Izzy." She paused. "Way before you had Porter come to me about Kelly."

"So, so why didn't you say anything?"

"Here's when I knew things were off. After I put you out I read the card that you gave me well before my mother told me that you told her about Alice. To my surprise that card told me all about how she bumped into you after you discovered her being locked up." Nine paused. "Kelly tried to pretend you just told her when she knew all along."

Isabel smiled.

"Thank you for helping me," Nine said. "I wanted my mother in my life so badly that I was willing to conform to the woman she was. Until I realized I didn't like the woman she was."

Isabel nodded. "It was mostly Porter. He was the one who brought me back into the house and kept me in his room. He was also the one who—"

"I already know," Nine said. "He betrayed them for me."

Isabel sat her cup down. “I’m serious, Nine. Porter went against his own mother and brother to protect you by giving you that information on the detective. And he got the info through Lisa.” She paused. “Both of them are really good people.”

“All the same,” Nine sighed. “Lisa’s beauty annoys me and I don’t know why.” Nine paused. “But are you sure it was just Kelly who tried to have me placed off the estate? Are you sure Bridget, Wagner and Lisa weren’t involved?”

“I’m certain of nothing but Porter did say Kelly was the one who went to the detective and that she told Wagner, Bridgette and Lisa. And that’s how he found out.”

“It doesn’t matter,” Nine said. “They’ll all be leaving soon anyway.”

“Are you sure it’s a good idea? I mean, with your wealth you need genuine people around you. That means me, Porter and Lisa.” She paused. “Plus if you send Lisa away Wagner will continue to abuse her and Kerrick II.”

“What do you mean abuse Kerrick II?”

“Wagner is a really terrible person, Nine,” Isabel said. “Please try and compromise and let them stay. I'll take full responsibility. I'm begging you."

NINE

Nine walked into the cell where Alice once lived and Kelly now stayed. "Just let me go." Kelly said gripping the bars. "This is crazy. I'm still your mother and don't deserve to be treated like this."

"If I do anything it won't be letting you go." Nine sat in the chair across from the cell.

"So you just gonna keep me in here like a prisoner?"

"No." Nine crossed her legs. "Won't be doing that either."

"Then what will you be doing?"

"I wanted to tell you some things about myself." Nine sighed. "Some things I want you to know about your daughter. Some things that everything that happened here made me realize lately." She paused. "I'm very smart."

"So you bragging now?"

"No, mother," she said softly. "That's the last thing I want or need to do. I just wanted you to know what kind of person I am. I wanted you to see that despite your best efforts you haven't succeeded in making me be, well, like you. And I wanted you to know these things before."

"Before what?"

"You die."

Kelly's eyes widened. "But why would you kill me?" Kelly pleaded. "I will go far away and never return. Just don't do this."

"What did you think would happen once you were found to be a snake?" She paused. "Huh? What did you think I would do? Your actions clearly showed that you have no idea how calculating I am. Do you realize how hard it was to be grandfather's most hated grandchild before rising to power and becoming his most prized? Nothing but a smart woman could rise to power in that short amount of time." She paused. "I'm nothing like you."

"Please, Nine." She begged. "Why won't you just let me go?"

"Because I don't trust my weakness of wanting your love if you ever returned."

Kelly looked down. It was obvious it was all over. She glared. “I pushed Jeremy off that ladder you know.”

Nine looked up and rose, walking slowly toward her. “What did you say?”

“I pushed him off that ladder,” she smiled sinisterly. “I overheard Bridget saying how special he was to her and I knew it was the only way to convince her to agree to go to the police and say you committed a crime. And it worked. I even went to him with the dumb idea to sing to you out the window.”

Nine was so angry she trembled.

“So you see, daughter, I’m not as dumb as you think.”

“But if that were true, why are you in there and I’m out here?” Nine released the .45 from the back of her pants. “Goodbye, mother.”

BOOM!

CHAPTER TWENTY-SEVEN

ANTONIUS

"Though this be madness, yet there is method in it..."

- William Shakespeare

Rain poured against the mansion as Nine sat in the sitting room when the doorbell rang. A few minutes later Bethany appeared with Antonius. "He couldn't get in so I brought him to you," Bethany said. "I hope that's okay."

"Yes, of course," Nine stood up when she saw his blood red eyes and scratched up face. "You can leave us, Bethany." When she was gone Nine moved closer. "Antonius, what's, what's wrong?"

Antonius shook his head softly. "You were right."

"About?"

"Alice."

Nine gasped. She worked so hard to correct all her mistakes and still she left one loose end out in the world. Nine never trusted Alice but she trusted Antonius to keep her safe by watching over her and now it appeared to be a mistake.

"Antonius...no." She whispered. "Please say it isn't so."

"I'm so sorry, Nine."

She backed up and fell into the sofa. With her hands clutched in front of her she asked, "Where is she?"

Silence.

"Antonius, please." She looked up at him. "Tell me where she is so I can send my men to find her before she comes for me."

"I killed her."

Nine exhaled, never realizing until that moment that she wasn't breathing. She knew her instincts said Alice was not to be trusted but now she was discovering that she was right about Antonius.

He was forever loyal.

She walked up to him and grabbed his hands. The same hands that had taken Alice's breath away. "Antonius, I'm so, so, so sorry. All I wanted was your happiness. No, I never trusted my cousin but I truly, truly wanted you to have your dream."

He nodded. "I know, and thank you." He took a deep breath. "I just wanted you to know that you're safe now. Goodbye, Nine." Broken hearted he turned to walk away when Nine walked in front of him and hugged him tightly. She didn't let him go until his tense body softened in her arms.

When she finally separated from him she increased her height by standing on her toes and kissing him gently. She could feel all additional stress leave him as if he were no longer weighed down by evil.

"Nine, I—"

She kissed him again.

"Nine, what about—"

She kissed him again.

"Nine, please listen to me. I have always loved you," he said. "But I don't want you to feel obligated to do this just because I'm—"

She kissed him once more.

This time their lips remained pressed together as his hand caressed her shoulders at first and then her arms, moving carefully alongside her waist. This was the moment of his dreams and yet it was happening in reality.

Lifting her up off her feet he slowly carried her to the sofa and lay her down. She motioned to remove the long black dress she wore until he said, "Please. I...I need to do this my way." He paused. "I need to...I need to savor this moment."

"Okay, Antonius," Nine smiled. "Do as you wish." She placed her arms over her head.

As if she were a precious gift he went to work carefully. First he slid his hands upward under the dress until it was over her head and on the floor. Her body gave him immediate chills. She was an impressive sight to behold and he didn't understand how Leaf, let alone any man could refuse her. "Wow." He said softly. "You're...you're better than I ever imagined."

"Why thank you." She winked.

Using the front latch he popped off her red lace bra and exhaled when he freed her breasts. "Nine, I knew you would be beautiful...but...breathtaking you are." His sentence was all over the place because he couldn't find the right words to describe her.

Exquisite was one word he could've used.

Looking downward he peeled off her panties next, gliding them downward slowly. She helped by raising each leg, opening up her pussy in the process. Seeing her this way his dick was so stiff it throbbed.

"You are everything." Lowering his head he spread her legs apart and ran his tongue over her pink button. The tip was slightly bitter and he licked her again as if doing so would save his life.

The passionate way he took care of her caused Nine to bite her bottom lip and moan. "Mmmmmm...that...oh my, God, you feel so good. Please, please don't stop."

Antonius had a secret.

He already came the moment he saw her body but he wasn't worried because already he was hard again. His tongue glided to the left of her clit and then the right with soft and fluid movements. Loving what he was doing, his mouth glistened like he was wearing lip-gloss as he continued to eat her pussy for points. He was doing it right too because she was transported and none of her troubles mattered.

"Oh, Antonius, I'm begging you please not to stop," she pled as she placed a hand on each side of his head and fucked his face softly. "You...um...mmm...my...goodness...I...I..." She bit down on her bottom lip again. "I'm...I'm cumming."

Before she released he eased up and entered her tight warm pussy. Pushing into her close to keep the pressure on her clit she exploded her cream all over his dick as he came again at the same time. “I…I’m cumming,” he said. “Mmmmmmmmm, that felt so, so good.” Trying to catch his breath he looked down at her. Now guilt weighed on his heart. “I’m so sorry that I just took…took advantage of you.”

She placed her hand on the side of his face. “You couldn’t take advantage of me if you tried.” She winked. “Plus you didn’t do anything to me that I didn’t want or need.”

He kissed her and she opened for him again neither knowing that Wagner hung in the background watching it all.

CHAPTER TWENTY-EIGHT

LEAF

"Cry havoc and let slip the dogs of war."

- William Shakespeare

Leaf wobbled up to the back door of Aristocrat Hills as rain pounded at his face. Nine instructed everyone in the mansion not to allow Leaf in the home, but neglected to inform the men on the gate. Now on the property and drunk out of his mind, he was trying to see Nine at once.

When he attempted to use his key to enter he realized all locks had been changed. Holding a half empty bottle of vodka and spilling it everywhere he yelled, "Nine, where are you? Open, open the fucking door! This is my house too! Don't make me burn this bitch down!"

Pulling his cell phone out of his pocket he tossed the bottle on the ground and dialed a number. "Chris...Chris," he said slurring. "I need you to come to the mansion. Bring five men."

"Yes, boss. We on the way." Leaf tossed the cell phone on the wet grass and grabbed the bottle off the ground but he could not be quenched because all the liquor had poured out.

"Fuck!" He yelled tossing the bottle away.

He was about to walk back to the U-Haul he rented that held his five dogs and wait for his men. He rented the vehicle because the last thing he needed was them barking at the house alone, especially after he just cleaned up behind the crime scene Nine left for him.

It wasn't Red's death that concerned Leaf. He never took her more seriously than their sexual encounters together. He was angrier that despite his best efforts he was still in love with Nine. And now since he had been caught cheating he was certain that he would cause her to run into the arms of Antonius, which was something he couldn't bare.

Deciding to wait on his men he turned around to walk to the U-Haul. But suddenly the door opened and Wagner walked out of it and into the rain. "Leaf!" He yelled. Leaf spun around. "You coming in or not? I have something to show you that you won't believe."

NINE

Nine and Antonius were in the shower looking into each other's eyes. Realizing that she was finally in his arms caused his body to quiver. Smiling down at her he said, "You don't have to worry. I already know."

"Know what?" She whispered.

"That you are still in love and that all we have is this moment." He paused. "I accept it gladly because even if I were to die right now I can truly say I lived."

She exhaled. "Thank you, Antonius. Thank you for being understanding." She paused. "Leaf he...he saved me at a dark time. And even though he cheated—"

"Wait, what are you talking about even though he cheated?" He frowned.

"He was sleeping with his neighbor and I found out about her."

Antonius didn't dare tell her that he had known about the woman too and didn't say a word. He just got into her graces *and* her body.

There was no way in hell he was letting Leaf destroy his shit.

"Wow, I'm sorry," he said as if he didn't know. "But I want you to know that I'm always here for you, Nine. I will lay down my life gladly even though we can't be together. All you have to do is say the word."

She touched the side of his face and kissed him softly. "I don't deserve you."

"You deserve me and more." He corrected her.

She took a deep breath. "Let's not talk about Leaf anymore. This moment is about us. I mean, Leaf's not thinking about me anyway. He made that clear. He just—"

"That's not true."

"What do you mean?"

"It's not true that Leaf doesn't love you." He paused. "Some men can't support a strong woman but you can take nothing from the fact that Leaf Prophet breathes for you. I'm certain of it."

"Wow. You have a pass to talk badly against him and still you don't."

"Why would I do that?" He paused. "Honor above all. Always."

Suddenly the door flew open and five men rushed inside. Antonius tried to make a beeline for his pants that sat on the toilet and held his gun but the bathroom was so large that it was too far away. Within seconds they were dragged out of the shower and thrown on the floor.

Leaf and Wagner walked inside and looked down at their wet naked bodies.

"Hello, love birds," Leaf said through clenched teeth. "Having fun in my pussy yet, nigga?" He brought down his Timberland boot on Antonius's face.

LEAF

Leaf ordered that Nine and Antonius be tied to wooden trellises while naked, the rain slapping at their faces while he looked on them with disdain. Behind him were five of his men, each holding one of his loud barking dogs.

Wagner stood next to them, smiling and thinking everything was funny. He had no idea that Nine's husband would be the way he would get at the estate for his mother and there he was, closer to having it all than he'd ever been before.

"You can do whatever you want to me but please don't hurt Nine," Antonius begged. "If you do you gonna regret it, man. I promise you. Just please...please don't hurt her."

"Niggas who fuck my wife ain't fit to say shit to me!" Leaf yelled like a wild animal.

"It was only once," Nine cried. "Only once. Please, please don't hurt us. I'll send Antonius away. I'll never talk to him again just please don't take his life."

Every time Nine spoke the dogs got louder as if they remembered her killing their brother some time ago to get revenge on Leaf.

"Shut up, bitch!" Leaf yelled. "Just shut the fuck up!" He paused. "You got the nerve to be giving my pussy away to this nigga and then you out here begging for his life? How you sound? Are you trying to make me kill EVERYBODY?"

"I knew she was a whore!" Wagner yelled.

Hearing his voice Leaf turned around and glared at him. "What you just say?"

"I said she was a whore."

Leaf nodded and...BOOM!

Wagner received a bullet to the back of his head by one of his men. Just as Lisa predicted. His body slumped forward and hit the ground.

"Sick of that nigga anyway." He looked at his men. "Get the ground beef out the bucket."

One of the men, while still holding the dog handed the leash to Leaf. Moving to the bucket he grabbed a huge chunk and then smeared the meat all over Antonius' body. Although most of the meat fell in heaps on the ground the dogs wouldn't care. His flesh would still hold the scent, which meant he would be edible.

Realizing what was happening Nine felt weak. "Oh my God no, Leaf!" Nine cried. "Don't do this! Please! Don't fucking do this!"

"Nine, it's okay," Antonius said calmly looking over at her despite what was about to happen. But her attention remained on Leaf, as she yelled and screamed, trying to do all she can to stop Antonius' fate. "Nine, look at me..." When she continued to cry he grew louder. "Nine Prophet, look at me right now!"

Finally she did.

"My time is over on this earth. So let me admit this. I am and have always been in love with you. And I will go to my death bed knowing that you are the one true love of my life." He paused. "I don't want you feeling any guilt about this. Because you gave me the best night of my life and I will die proudly."

"This nigga really disrespecting now." Hearing Antonius' words angered him so much he turned to his men and said, "Release the hounds!"

Now off the leash and with loud snarling growls, the animals lunged toward the meat on the ground first. But when it was gone, and they still hadn't gotten their fill, they sniffed around Antonius.

But suddenly something happened.

The black lab with the grey stripe running down his head got in front of Antonius, protecting him from his brothers and mother. The animal sensed that Antonius was good and somewhere in his soul knew he was the one responsible for bringing him into this world.

Every time one of his brothers or his mother tried to snap at Antonius' flesh the dog would snap back. Leaf, seeing this shit grew more agitated. First his woman was protecting him now his animal.

What was becoming of the world?

Leaf glared. "It figures. There's always one disloyal ass bitch out the bunch."

Tiring of the scene he raised his gun and shot the dog in the neck causing him to lay flat. At first the animals were scared but they were ravenous and hungry since they hadn't eaten. With bearing teeth they rushed Antonius stepping over their dead brother in the process. Gnawing at his legs they didn't stop until they were able to pull off slats of his flesh in mounds. Antonius screamed out in pain as they continued to tear into him until his skin opened and blood poured out into the vineyard.

Hearing Antonius' wails, Nine closed her eyes as he was yanked from the trellis. Soon he grew silent and all could be heard were the animal's snarls as they feasted.

Nine wept softly.

Still chained to thick wooden trellises used to upkeep the vineyard behind Aristocrat Hills, she begged for mercy from all who would listen. Still completely naked, blood oozed from her beaten face, arms and thighs deepening the redness of the grapes surrounding her chocolate frame. Ever so often lightning flashed across the sky brightening her beautiful but pummeled features; as thunder appeared to yell *fuck you* from above.

Through swollen eyes she could see that it was obvious that Leaf was not there to offer mercy, but to enact the brand of revenge he felt she deserved.

Taking a deep breath Nine looked above and said, "So this is really it for me."

"Shouldn't it be?" Leaf asked, pointing the barrel of a .45 at her as if it were a microphone. "Don't play the martyr, Nine. You have also killed many."

Her head hung low upon hearing the words. "This may be true. But it was always within the rules of the game. But this is different."

"Shut the fuck up!" He grew louder. "Just shut up!"

Nine sighed deeply. "If this is it, let me say I'm sorry now for all the things I wanted to be for my sons but couldn't. And that if this be my final resting place then I will accept my fate because I am at home. But trust me, it may not be now or even this year, but you will soon receive yours." She glared.

As she looked outward, the pain of the betrayal she felt in her heart thickened by Leaf, whose blood coursed through her veins and whose heart she thought she owned, she took a deep breath.

Realizing her fate, and with a resilience only Nine Prophet could muster she said, "If you're going to do it let's get it over with, nigga. I will beg no more."

He walked up to her and rubbed the gun alongside her cheek. "You belong to me and you made me become this."

"Whatever, Leaf," she said softly. "It doesn't matter any—"

BOOM!

When Leaf turned around he saw one of his men on the ground while Isabel, still dressed in the habit, stood behind another man holding a gun to the back of his head. That quickly she already killed one of his men and was threatening to end the life of another. His dogs, now full, took off running upon hearing the gunshot. The animals weren't crazy enough to end up like their dead brother.

"I will blow his head off if you don't cut her down now!" Isabel promised.

Leaf laughed. "I wasn't going to hurt Nine. I was—"

BOOM!

She shot another and moved to the next man. "I'm not fucking around. Cut her down! Now!"

"Okay, okay, okay," he said tucking his gun in the back of his pants. He looked at one of his remaining three men and said, "Cut her down."

One of the men quickly ran to fulfill the request. When her limp weak body fell to the ground he picked her up and held her in his arms. Isabel was so caught up in seeing to it that Nine was free that she didn't see the two remaining men looking at each other with disdain. Before she could dispute they ambushed her, snatching the gun from her hand.

"Boss, what do you want us to do with this bitch?" One of them asked while holding her with a forearm to the neck. He was livid that he had already lost two of his friends and eager to return the favor.

"If you kill her," Nine said out of breath to Leaf, "You might as well kill me too because it is over."

Leaf looked at Isabel closely and grinned.

LEAF

Leaf gazed at Nine who lie sideways on their bed, still shocked silent by Antonius' gruesome murder. She'd done and seen some vile things in her lifetime but never to a man she loved so much. "Why, Leaf?" She whispered. "Having known him can you honestly say he deserved that type of fate?"

"If we didn't work out he was the next in line to be with you. And I'm not gonna live a life where I have a nigga in competition for my wife."

She shook her head. "But he was kind, Leaf. And loyal."

"And you rewarded him by fucking him!"

"And you fucked her too!" She sat up.

"And you rewarded her by taking her life," Leaf said. "All's fair in sex and bullets isn't it?"

Nine glared. "I will never forgive you for this, Leaf. Ever."

"I don't want your forgiveness. I demand your love."

Nine eased off the bed, stood up and grabbed her robe off the chair. "You always said I was violent but look at what the Prophet blood created. You are a living, breathing monster."

He laughed.

She slid on her robe.

Preparing to walk out he grabbed one of her wrists gently. "Do you still love me?"

She stared at him for what seemed like forever. "Sadly. The answer is still yes." She stormed out.

LISA

Nine was brushing her hair in the mirror when Lisa walked into her room. "Nine." She paused. "Can I talk to you for a minute?"

Nine nodded. "Yes. Of course." She put her brush down on the vanity and faced her.

"Do you like me?"

Nine sighed. "I haven't made a decision yet. But Isabel seems to take to you. Which is why I have agreed to let you and your son live here for now. Along with Porter." She paused. "It is true right? That your son was being abused by his father."

"No."

Nine's eyebrows rose. "I mean yes Wagner was abusing him and me but Wagner was not his father. It was daddy."

Nine shook her head. "Wow. The more time goes on the more I'm coming to realize that he was a real monster." She exhaled. "I will always respect our culture to have the option to breed amongst ourselves to keep the money in the family, but no child will have sex thrust upon them. Everyone must choose when they are of age. And if they don't that's fine too." Nine took a deep breath. "I just have to stop all of this pain."

"That brings me to my next statement. I wanted to tell you that I don't want to live by the Prophet ways anymore."

"You mean choosing a mate within the family?"

"Yes."

Nine took a deep breath. "You know I realized something about our ways. It's not about what we do it's that our family history is so dark no one will understand but another Prophet. I mean, how can you find someone who won't think we are all mad?"

"I met someone already."

Nine's eyes widened. "Really."

"Yes and I'm in love." She paused. "I mean it will work because my situation is complicated and his situation is complicated too."

"Why?"

"He's married."

"Married?" Nine didn't approve. "What is his name?"

"Rasim. Rasim Nami."

Nine gasped. "Oh my God."

EPILOGUE

Nine sat at one end of the long dining room table and Leaf on the other. The chandelier glowed a soft yellow over their heads causing them both to glisten. Dressed in all red like Bloods, they sat across from each other, medium well steaks and cauliflower with cheese before them.

"The meal is good," Leaf said.

"Compliments to the chef." She responded.

Over the months both Leaf and Nine occupied the same house although not the same room. On Nine's corridor were Isabel, Lisa, Porter, Bethany, Noel, Samantha, the children and the refugees. And on Leaf's corridor were himself and his dogs.

Refusing to speak or sleep together except when they shared a meal nightly, both Leaf and Nine also made it certain that neither would be with another person sexually or emotionally if they could help it, which they did. And since word had gotten out that they could be violent to anyone who came into the cousins' relationship, people steered clear of them.

The emotional tension as well as the sexual tension was high but Nine never forgave him for sleeping with Red and killing Antonius. And Leaf never forgave her for giving her body and part of her heart to Antonius.

So they became this microcosm of hate and love that could explode at any moment.

Isabel once referred to this future boiling point as a real life *War Of The Roses*, based off the movie with the same name. Where if they couldn't get along they would kill themselves and each other in the process.

And those who lived in Aristocrat Hills believed she was right.

"You look beautiful," he said.

"Fuck you."

He grinned. "You're making me want you even more, Nine."

"You'll never get this pussy again."

He wiped his mouth with the black linen napkin in his lap. With his looks back now that he pushed back on the drinking, he was a snack. "Is that right?"

Silence.

Slowly he rose and moved toward her as if he had all the time in the world. When he finally made it to her end of the table he stared down at her with delight. Her breath quickened because they hadn't been that close to one another in almost eight months. Looking down at her he said, "Open your legs, Nine."

"I'm not—"

"Open your fucking legs," he yelled grabbing her silky hair which now reached her shoulders and pulling backwards.

She smiled and opened slowly, causing the suspense to kill him. Lowering his height, he moved the chair roughly until he was on his knees and between her legs. "No panties huh?"

"Since you're here less talking. And more eating."

Snaking his hands behind her he grabbed each ass cheek and pulled until his face was nestled in her pussy. His tongue first took the trip in her tunnel and then rolled up to her clit lapping repeatedly. She had already begun the glistening process the moment Leaf walked her way but now she was all oil.

Pawning a head full of his black curly hair, she wiggled her chocolate pussy all over his vanilla colored lips until she was almost there.

"Fuck that shit," he said rising up after tasting her sweet cream. "You gonna suck this dick first."

Looking down at her, he undid his Louis Vuitton belt and then unzipped his pants. Pushing down his silk boxers she took his dick into her palms. "If you bite me I will kill you," he warned.

"That's the chance you have to take."

After not touching his wife in almost a year he was gladly willing to take the chance and the risk was worth the reward. Nine ran her tongue alongside his creamy colored pole until Leaf's head flew back. "Fuck," he moaned. "I forgot how good you fucking feel."

When he glanced down at her she gave him a sinister look and it turned him on even more. "Hands on the table, bitch." He knocked her plate onto the floor. "You about to get this dick."

In the submissive mood, Nine stood up, bent forward and assumed the position. Pushing her down he made sure her belly was flat on the table and her ass was up in the air. Kicking her legs apart as if he were police, he stuffed her until she was full.

Leaf banged and banged until Nine was shivering. She had cum seconds earlier and he noticed but it didn't mean she wasn't enjoying the ride.

"This pussy is still right, cousin," he said continuing to pound into her.

"I'm glad you like it," she moaned.

He didn't stop pounding her until he couldn't take it anymore and exploded into her pink pussy.

When he was done he grabbed a linen napkin off the floor and wiped his dick. Afterwards Nine wiped the corners of her mouth, pulled her dress down and sat down, scooting up to the table.

Leaf strutted toward the other end and took a seat too. Both performing as if nothing happened.

Now looking across from each other he yelled, "Maria, we're ready for dessert."

Nine grinned. "This isn't over, cousin. I still hate you."

"Of course not," he replied. "War is never over until there is but one man standing."

TO READ ABOUT THE REFUGEES READ

NEFARIOUS

TO READ ABOUT RASIM NAMI READ

PRISON THRONE

PROPHET FAMILY TREE

TIMELINE OF BIRTHS

THE ORIGINAL PROPHETS

1953 – Kerrick is born

1976 – Kelly is born

1977 – 2nd CHILD – Avery is born

1978 – 3rd CHILD – Marina is born

1979 – 4th CHILD – Victory is born

1980 – 5th CHILD – Justin is born

1992 – Kelly and Avery's Child – Lydia is born. (Killed by a car)

- Paige is born. (Murdered later by Nine)

1993 – Marina and Joshua Saint's Child – Alice is born.

1994 – Victory and Blake's Child – Noel is born.

1995 – Victory and Blake's Child – Samantha is born.

1996 - Victory and Blake's Child - Isabel is born.

1997 – Victory and Blake's Child – Bethany is born.

1997 – Kelly and Avery's Child - Karen is born. (Deformed. Murdered by Kerrick.)

- Corrine and Justin's Child – Autumn (Leaf) is born.

1998 – Kelly and Avery's Child - Nine is Born.

2014 – Julius is Born to Paige – Raised by Nine

2016 – Leaf and Nine's Child - Miscarried due to close bloodline due to incest.

2017 – Leaf and Nine's Child – Magnus Prophet

TIMELINE OF BIRTHS
THE ILLEGITIMENT PROPHETS

1992 - Kerrick and Bridget's Child - Lisa is born.

1993 – Kerrick and Bridget's Triplets – Wagner, Porter and Jeremy are born.

2012 – Lisa and Wagner's Child – Kerrick II is born.

The Cartel Publications Order Form

www.thecartelpublications.com

Inmates **ONLY** receive novels for $10.00 per book.

(Mail Order **MUST** come from inmate directly to receive discount)

Title	Qty	Price
Shyt List 1		$15.00
Shyt List 2		$15.00
Shyt List 3		$15.00
Shyt List 4		$15.00
Shyt List 5		$15.00
Pitbulls In A Skirt		$15.00
Pitbulls In A Skirt 2		$15.00
Pitbulls In A Skirt 3		$15.00
Pitbulls In A Skirt 4		$15.00
Pitbulls In A Skirt 5		$15.00
Victoria's Secret		$15.00
Poison 1		$15.00
Poison 2		$15.00
Hell Razor Honeys		$15.00
Hell Razor Honeys 2		$15.00
A Hustler's Son		$15.00
A Hustler's Son 2		$15.00
Black and Ugly		$15.00
Black and Ugly As Ever		$15.00
Year Of The Crackmom		$15.00
Deadheads		$15.00
The Face That Launched A Thousand Bullets		$15.00
The Unusual Suspects		$15.00
Miss Wayne & The Queens of DC		$15.00
Paid In Blood (eBook Only)		$15.00
Raunchy		$15.00
Raunchy 2		$15.00
Raunchy 3		$15.00
Mad Maxxx		$15.00
Quita's Dayscare Center		$15.00
Quita's Dayscare Center 2		$15.00
Pretty Kings		$15.00
Pretty Kings 2		$15.00
Pretty Kings 3		$15.00
Pretty Kings 4		$15.00
Silence Of The Nine		$15.00
Silence Of The Nine 2		$15.00
Silence Of The Nine 3		$15.00
Prison Throne		$15.00
Drunk & Hot Girls		$15.00
Hersband Material		$15.00
The End: How To Write A Bestselling Novel In 30 Days (Non-Fiction Guide)		$15.00
Upscale Kittens		$15.00
Wake & Bake Boys		$15.00
Young & Dumb		$15.00
Young & Dumb 2:		$15.00
Tranny 911		$15.00
Tranny 911: Dixie's Rise		$15.00

First Comes Love, Then Comes Murder ________	$15.00
Luxury Tax ________	$15.00
The Lying King ________	$15.00
Crazy Kind Of Love ________	$15.00
And They Call Me God ________	$15.00
The Ungrateful Bastards ________	$15.00
Lipstick Dom ________	$15.00
A School of Dolls ________	$15.00
Hoetic Justice ________	$15.00
KALI: Raunchy Relived ________	$15.00
Skeezers ________	$15.00
You Kissed Me, Now I Own You ________	$15.00
Nefarious ________	$15.00
Redbone 3: The Rise of The Fold ________	$15.00
The Fold ________	$15.00
Clown Niggas ________	$15.00
The One You Shouldn't Trust ________	$15.00
The WHORE The Wind Blew My Way ________	$15.00
She Brings The Worst Kind ________	$15.00
The House That Crack Built ________	$15.00
The House That Crack Built 2 ________	$15.00
The House That Crack Built 3 ________	$15.00

(**Redbone 1** & **2** are **NOT** Cartel Publications novels and if **ordered** the cost is **FULL** price of $15.00 **each**. **No Exceptions**.)

Please add $5.00 **PER BOOK** for shipping and handling.

The Cartel Publications * P.O. BOX 486 OWINGS MILLS MD 21117

Name: ________________________

Address: ________________________

City/State: ________________________

Contact/Email: ________________________

Please allow 7-10 BUSINESS days before shipping.

The Cartel Publications is NOT responsible for Prison Orders rejected!

NO RETURNS and NO REFUNDS.

NO PERSONAL CHECKS ACCEPTED

STAMPS NO LONGER ACCEPTED

MAY 1 0 2019

CPSIA information can be obtained
at www.ICGtesting.com
Printed in the USA
LVHW042313110419
613929LV00001B/59